F
Ang   Angell, Judie
         First the good news

DATE DUE			
OCT 0 4 1984			
OCT 1 2 1984			
Dec 19			
Ap. 23			
FEB 0 5 1988			

First
The Good News

ALSO BY JUDIE ANGELL

Dear Lola
or How to Build Your Own Family

A Word from Our Sponsor
or My Friend Alfred

The Buffalo Nickel Blues Band

In Summertime It's Tuffy

Tina Gogo

What's Best for You

Ronnie and Rosey

Secret Selves

Suds

First
The Good News

By Judie Angell

BRADBURY PRESS   SCARSDALE, NEW YORK

Bradbury Press, Inc.
2 Overhill Road
Scarsdale, N.Y. 10583
An affiliate of Macmillan, Inc.
Collier Macmillan Canada, Inc.
Manufactured in the United States of America
10 9 8 7 6 5 4 3 2 1
The text of this book is set in 11 pt. Janson.
Library of Congress Cataloging in Publication Data
Angell, Julie.
First the good news.
Summary: Ninth-grade journalist Annabelle Goobitz and her four best friends pretend to be groupies in order to land an interview with television comedian Hap Rhysbeck, but the young comedian makes an announcement that takes them by surprise.
[1. Journalism—Fiction.   2. Comedians—Fiction.   3. Television—Fiction]
I. Title.
PZ7.A5824Fi   1983   [Fic]   83-6074
ISBN 0-02-705820-4

This is for
Kendra and Lindsay
from their loving aunt

First
The Good News

1...

Annabelle Goobitz hated her name until her thirteenth birthday. On that day she began to sing its syllables while snapping her fingers, letting the accents fall where they might. Hearing An-NA-belle Goo-BITZ or An-na-BELLE GOO-bitz in Latin or rock beats helped her decide that she could be anything she wanted to be. Whatever that was. She didn't know yet. But she'd be famous. Someday the world would be snapping its fingers to the Annabelle Goobitz beat.

Her four best friends, who with Annabelle comprised the girls' club they called "Adam's Ribbers," didn't know

1

what they would be either, but they were less concerned than Annabelle with long-range goals. They were concerned mostly with what color their club sweaters should be. They had already decided on collegiate-looking cardigans with two stripes on the left upper arm, but the colors were the subject of endless discussions.

Adam's Ribbers met on Monday afternoons at Annabelle's apartment and Wednesday afternoons at Helaine Jacoby's. They also met more informally in the girls' room at school whenever they could all get passes from class at the same time, at any of seven or eight shops or hangouts downtown on the weekends and at any other time that Shirley Ferguson didn't have a violin lesson or Helaine, Weight Watchers. The five had been the closest of friends since they had all been in the same fifth-grade homeroom, and the class bully had kidded Helaine about her weight. Annabelle had stood up and lectured him, while Dorothy Pevney offered some incisive comments regarding his intelligence. Josephine Scarangillo had hit him with her bookbag and Shirley Ferguson gave a rousing "Yeah!" after everything the other girls said. From that time on they were all inseparable.

But they hadn't formed a club until the beginning of junior high. At that point, Annabelle decided they should prove to the world that they weren't just a bunch of frivolous children, but an organized group, working for the common good.

"*Whose* common good?" Josephine Scarangillo wanted to know.

2

"Mankind's," Annabelle answered grandly. "The common good of mankind."

"That's neat," Shirley Ferguson said.

So in seventh grade, they began to hold formal meetings in which to organize their various projects.

After three months, the only project they could agree on was the adoption of a family from the *New York Times'* list of One Hundred Neediest Cases which was printed every year around Christmas time. That was all right, except that because they weren't allowed to get to know the family personally, Annabelle felt the "human element" was missing.

"They *are* human, Annabelle," Dorothy said. "I mean, we *know* it's a human family."

"But we don't know them," Annabelle complained, "and they don't know us."

"Well, so what? We know we're helping someone, that's the point."

"Not the way we could if we knew them," Annabelle insisted.

"I think maybe you just want to be thanked, Annabelle," Josephine said. "Now, come on, isn't that it?"

"That is the grossest thing you ever said, Jo," Annabelle responded. "That's not it at all. What I meant was, if we met the family, then we'd know all the personal things, like what styles the girls liked and what kinds of toys the baby liked, or what the mother needed for the kitchen . . . Even the foods they—"

"Now, look," Josephine interrupted. "We have their sizes and all their ages, now all we have to do is scrounge up enough nice clothes and shoes and things to get them all through the winter and—"

"But—"

"No buts, Annabelle. Now the paper said that what they really want most is winter clothes, so that's what we'll get them and they'll be happy and *we'll* be happy, okay?"

"We'd all be happier if we could get to know them and read to the kids and baby-sit and take them to the playground and stuff like that . . ."

"Annabelle," Dorothy said, "we're not adopting them for*ever*, you know, that's not the deal. Only for Christmas, that's *all*. I'm only twelve years old and I'm not ready to adopt an entire family for the rest of my life. My mother won't even let me adopt a kitten from the humane society, Annabelle!"

Annabelle sighed and moaned, Dorothy and Josephine argued and joked and Shirley and Helaine went out and got most of the clothes for the needy family. That had been their seventh-grade project.

In eighth grade, they cooked a Thanksgiving dinner for a downtown soup kitchen and sang Christmas carols at a home for the elderly. They had thought about being candy stripers at the hospital, but Dorothy said that the thought of bedpans made her violently ill and Helaine said that if the stripes on the uniforms ran horizontally she'd look too fat. They also joined the staff of the school newspaper and wrote numerous columns concerning illegal aliens, the Middle East crisis, the nuclear arms race, the state of the poor in the South Bronx, euthanasia,

4

women's rights, air pollution and the plight of stray animals. The paper actually printed two of the columns.

Now, in ninth grade, their final junior-high year, Annabelle wanted to go out in style.

One Wednesday afternoon in early fall, after Helaine's mother had served brownies and milk to all the girls except Helaine, they began their usual squabble about the agenda.

"Well, how about the club project first?" Helaine suggested.

"Let's get the sweater colors over with," Josephine said. "If we're going to get sweaters, let's get them. By the time we decide it'll be summer and too hot to wear them."

"I've been thinking . . ." Annabelle said, and Dorothy sighed. "I think our project this year should *say* something to the world."

"Say what, Annabelle?" Shirley asked. She adored Annabelle and everyone else who expressed an opinion first.

"We'll all be married by the time we get sweaters," Josephine said with a sigh.

Annabelle continued. "I think we should say to the world that we're important. And that we have something to say. After all, it's our future the world is messing up, isn't it? Shouldn't we have a say in it? I think we should use the school paper, too. We are the senior staffers this year, and it'll be harder to reject us now. When we move to the high school, we'll be on the lowest rung again."

"Use the paper for what, Annabelle?" Helaine asked. "I mean, we've tried, but the five of us simply can't stop the arms race. What do you want to use the paper for?"

Annabelle slumped down. "I don't know," she said. "But something."

"Can we take a break?" Dorothy said. "I have got something that will absolutely knock your socks off."

"What?" Shirley asked. "What is it?"

"Well . . ." Dorothy reached into her schoolbag. "I've been saving this as a surprise for when we were all together again. It's an album of comedy routines from "Live From Sound Stage 3." Jo, you'll honestly die! You all will!"

The girls grinned. "Live From Sound Stage 3" was one of the most popular television shows in the country with high-school and college kids. It was on late every Saturday night and the Adam's Ribbers loved to arrange slumber parties so they could all watch it together. The show had made a household word of one of its stars, Hap Rhysbeck.

"Wait until after the meeting, Dottie . . ." Annabelle said, but not too strongly. She was a big fan of the show. She felt it belonged to her, to all of them, and was out of the range of Adults. With a capital.

Dorothy moved toward the stereo. "You have to hear this," she was saying. "I just can't think about sweaters and projects until I know you all love this as much as I do. You have to share comedy, you know, you can't love it all by yourself."

"Is there a lot of Hap Rhysbeck on it?" Shirley asked.

Dorothy clutched the album to her chest. "Of course!" she cried. "I wouldn't have bought it if there weren't. Is he the most adorable thing you ever saw?"

"Well, but it's his humor," Annabelle said. "The way he looks at things. He makes you laugh at serious stuff. I love that."

"Remember last Saturday night?" Josephine asked and began to giggle. ". . . When he played a reporter sent out to cover the end of the world?"

Dorothy squealed. "He was afraid they left the studio without enough film in the camera?"

"And then . . ." Annabelle was grinning, ". . . they counted down the seconds until the end of the world, just like they do on New Year's Eve . . ."

" 'Five . . . four . . . three . . . two . . . one . . . And that's it, viewers. It's all over, the world has ended, after all the talk and worry and warnings, it is finally done. Finished. Kaput. Let this serve as a lesson to all of us. It *can* happen here. This is Hap Rhysbeck, S.S.3 News. Back to you, Jim.' "

Annabelle's nose wrinkled as she chuckled to herself. "He's really crazy," she said.

"Gorgeous, too," Dorothy added. "Now listen. This is terrific."

They played the album, nudging each other and stifling their laughter so as not to miss the next words.

"Oh, it's great, Dorothy!" Shirley cried when side one was over.

"I love the commercials!" Josephine giggled. "Don't you love those takeoffs they do on commercials?"

"I liked the interview with the author, the one with the bad temper," Helaine said. "That was terrific!"

"No, the one with the President on the psychiatrist's couch," Annabelle said. "That was the best."

"I just love Hap," Dorothy sighed. "Anything he says or does knocks me out!"

"Well . . ." Annabelle said, getting up from the floor, "I think we ought to get back to business."

Josephine said, "Okay. I want powder blue and white. It goes great with red hair."

"Let's think about a project," Annabelle said. "Where are our priorities? I *mean!*"

"I'd like to hear side two of the record," Helaine said.

"Oooh," Shirley said, "me too."

Josephine raised her hand and spoke at the same time. "Before you flip it, Dorothy, is powder blue and white okay with everyone? We can get our order in this week . . ."

"How about navy blue and maroon?" Dorothy asked.

"Maroon is awful with red hair!" Josephine wailed.

Annabelle threw up her hands. "I give up!" she cried. "I can see I'll have to do this myself. Play the record, Dot. All anybody cares about is being entertained!"

Annabelle stayed at Helaine's after the three others had left, grumbling as she picked at brownie crumbs.

"Come on, Annabelle," Helaine said cheerfully. "You know you loved it. You laughed as hard as anyone. Except maybe Dorothy . . ."

"Oh, I did," Annabelle answered. "It's just that we

always have so much fun we never seem to accomplish anything!"

She stretched out on the rug and began to bicycle in the air with her legs.

"Don't do that," Helaine said. "You make me feel guilty."

"I have all this energy!" Annabelle cried, leaping to her feet. "And no place to *put* it! I feel like a bomb somebody planted somewhere. I can even hear myself ticking!"

"Hmmm, that's funny," Helaine said from deep in her chair. "It's just the opposite with me. I always have this feeling I'm not getting enough sleep."

"What I want," Annabelle said, "is to do something noteworthy. Something that says look, here's Annabelle Goobitz and she's a go-getter, she's a dynamo, she can save the world. Or something."

Helaine yawned.

"Come on, Helaine, let's run around the block," Annabelle said.

"Oh, please, let's not," Helaine moaned. "Why do you have these feelings, Annabelle? I don't have them . . . Jo just wants to order sweaters, Dot wants to laugh at Hap Rhysbeck, Shirley's just happy tagging along . . . I mean, it's not that I don't admire you, Annabelle, really, it's just that I don't understand you!"

"Mmmm," Annabelle murmured, staring over Helaine's head at the window. "Maybe I just feel like too small a frog in too big a pond. I mean, look out the window, Helaine. What do you see?"

"The building next door," Helaine answered.

9

"Right. That's all I see from my apartment window, too. Buildings full of people, thousands and millions of people. Maybe if we lived in a small town I'd feel differently, but I just don't want to get lost in the maze. Y'know? Out there . . . you can *do* things. What is the thing you'd like to do most? I mean, if you could pick anything!"

"Lose twenty pounds!" Helaine answered instantly.

"You think small, Helaine."

"I know . . . I'd like to *be* small."

"I think about my parents," Annabelle went on. "They work hard all the time, running the deli—they're there day and night, just about, and what do they get?"

"A good living . . . and excellent pastrami," Helaine answered. "I don't know how you stay thin."

With a sigh, Annabelle put on her jacket and picked up her books. "Guess I'd better head down there," she said, "and help out a little. But I'm serious about making a mark, Helaine . . . I just have to think of a way to do it."

2...

When Annabelle was born, the first words her mother said to her father were, "Well, Lenny, it's another girl and I'm sorry, but that's it. I'm not trying again."

And Annabelle's father had replied in one breath, "It's okay, Miriam, I'm happy with her, she cries louder than any of the rest of 'em, she'll be fine, she'll be okay."

Annabelle was the youngest of four Goobitz daughters. She learned quickly how to fight for toys, food and attention. She was too young at the time to realize she had been born into an era that loudly proclaimed daughters were every bit as good as sons, but it wouldn't have mattered to Annabelle anyway. She already knew that. She had a gene for it.

The twins, Rosalyn and Rebecca, who were six when Annabelle was born, became her devoted slaves. Before she was a year old, Annabelle was yelling, "Rozzy—get *milk!*" and "Becca—get *doll!*" And they got them, while Miriam, their mother, puckered her lips and shook her head.

But if she had been only demanding, Annabelle would probably have lost favor rather quickly. She had an especially endearing quality which her father liked to call "charm" and which he later called "charisma," updating his vocabulary to the current fashion.

"When—my—baby—smiles at me," he would sing, and Annabelle would grin, dimpling her cheeks, as she clapped her pudgy hands. Even Miriam melted at Annabelle's smile. And when Susannah, the oldest and nine years older than Annabelle, caught her baby sister wearing her favorite sweater as a dress, she couldn't help laughing and took Annabelle's picture with her own Polaroid.

And as Annabelle grew older, she turned out to be the best helper in the family business—Goobitz's Good Bits—Delicatessen Supreme. Rosalyn also enjoyed helping at the deli but her sandwiches didn't get quite the praise that Annabelle's did from faithful customers and even from strangers.

"Let the little one with the braids make mine," the customers would say, or, "Only Annabelle has the right touch."

"She puts in too much," Rosalyn complained. "She stuffs them too full."

"No, I don't," Annabelle would answer. "It's the way you layer it. You have to bring it right to the ends of the bread, so they never get a mouthful of bread and no meat. I put in the same amount you do. Look, I'll show you." And she showed Rosalyn, but everyone still asked especially for Annabelle's pastrami.

Now, Rosalyn was the only other Goobitz sister at home. Susannah, twenty-three, was in Chicago, a buyer for a big chain store, and Becca was a junior at Syracuse University, studying fine arts. Rosalyn hadn't wanted college, she'd wanted to run the deli and that's what she had done, with her parents, since her graduation from high school. Though Annabelle was still the undeclared Sandwich Master, Rosalyn made platters and gift packages that could rival even the most experienced caterers'. Rosalyn's tempting trays of deli delights were works of art.

Now she looked up from behind the counter as the little bell over the door rang brightly and Annabelle came in.

"Hi," Rosalyn greeted her. "Wanna relieve me? Dad's in the back. Mom went home."

"Sure. Not too busy, is it?"

"Uh-uh. Been like this all day. Real quiet. How was the meeting?"

"We listened to an album. 'Live From Sound Stage 3.' "

"There's an album? I didn't know that."

"It's Dorothy's. She's in love with Hap Rhysbeck."

13

"Who isn't? Was it funny?"

"Mmmm . . ."

"Sounds like a veritable riot."

"No, it was. Really. I was just thinking . . ."

"Okay. You think. I'm leaving. Here's a pound of that coffee blend we grind for Mrs. Cagney. Her husband'll be in to pick it up. Want dinner here or home?"

"Here . . . I'll stay till closing and come home with Pop . . ."

"See ya!" Rosalyn hung up her apron and waved cheerfully to Annabelle on her way out the door.

The following afternoon, the girls stayed after school to attend a meeting of the James K. Polk Junior High School newspaper, *Weathervane*. They discovered that not too many of the regular staff was there.

"It's an advertising meeting, girls," the editor, Sammy Prysock, explained. "But stick around. I think advertising could use some new blood."

The girls shrugged at each other and took seats at the back.

Sammy began the meeting by tapping his pencil on the front desk.

"We don't have our advisor here today," Sammy began. "Mr. Hedley had another meeting. But I don't think we need him for this business . . ."

"We don't nccd ol' Headless at all!" Vic DeMarr, the sports editor, called out.

"Oh, Vic . . ." Dorothy whispered to Helaine. "He always has a comment about everything."

"What's he doing here anyway," Helaine whispered back, "if this is an advertising meeting? He does sports."

"Vic DeMarr shows up everywhere," Dorothy said with a wave of her fingers. "There's one in every crowd."

Sammy Prysock was still tapping his pencil. "We don't seem to be getting the same number of ads we managed to get last year," he said, and turned to the advertising manager, a boy named Howard Caswell. "Howard, you were supposed to sell an ad to Richter's Rexall and I don't see it here. They advertised in every issue last year. What's going on?"

"Mr. Richter said he wanted to change his old ad. He said he'd get back to me."

"Howard, don't wait for him to get back to you," Sammy said. "Nag him. Stay on his case. We need more ads. Then we can have more pages."

"Yeah, I need more room for my sports," Vic complained. "My whole track thing was cut last issue."

Helaine said to Dorothy, "Sammy should put Jo into selling ads. She'd be great at it."

"Mm," Dorothy agreed. "Howard's too sweet for it. One look at those basset-hound eyes of his and people know they've got a pushover."

"—more people to work with Howard," Sammy Prysock was saying. "Any suggestions?"

"You do it, Jo!" Helaine called to Josephine two seats away.

"Me?"

"She'd be great at it, Sammy. You would, Jo."

"Yeah, she helped her cousin Fred sell space for his college newsletter last year," Dorothy added.

"Okay, Jo?" Sammy asked.

"All right. But can I have help?"

"I'll help," Dorothy said, and Shirley added, "Me too."

"Great," Sammy said. "That's one problem off my back. Now you all can go except Sylvia Goldberg—you're doing the Roving Reporter column this issue, right, Sylvia?—and any of the layout people who are here. That's all. Thanks."

People began to file out of the room.

"Listen, Annabelle," Josephine said, grabbing her arm. "How about an ad from Goobitz's Good Bits next issue?"

"You sure don't waste any time," Annabelle said.

"Right," Jo agreed. "How about it?"

"Well, I guess my dad could take an ad," Annabelle said. "He took six last year."

"Great. And maybe Helaine could ask her Weight Watchers group."

"No," Helaine said firmly. "I don't want other kids from Polk joining up. They'll all find out just how much I weigh."

"Don't be silly, Helaine," Josephine told her. "They'll be there for the same reason. You'll know how much they weigh, too."

"Oh. That's true. I never thought of that."

16

"See? Two ads in two minutes. It's easy," Josephine said and clapped her hands. "Coming, Dot? We'll canvass the block on our way home."

"Okay," Dorothy agreed. "I want to stop at the T-shirt store and get a Hap Rhysbeck poster. You girls coming?"

"I am," Shirley said.

"No . . . I'm exhausted. I'm going home to take a nap," Helaine said. "What about you, Annabelle?"

"I think I'll wait until Sammy's finished in there. I want to talk to him."

"I know you, Annabelle," Josephine said, grinning. "You want to push some story ideas, right? What is it this time?"

"Well, I was thinking about a series on military spending."

Josephine patted her arm. "Save your breath, Annabelle," she said.

"Here it is!" Dorothy cried. "Oh, it's a great one, isn't it?" She held up the Hap Rhysbeck poster. It showed the television star in a "Sound Stage 3" T-shirt and tight jeans, grinning at a white cat draped over his left shoulder. "I'm going to get two," Dorothy said, picking another rolled cardboard cylinder out of a barrel.

"She has a room the size of a stamp and she's getting two posters," Josephine said to Shirley. "I think our Dottie has a crush. What do you think?"

"Isn't he married?" Shirley asked.

Dorothy whirled. *"What?"* she cried.

"No, he's not married," Jo said. "Calm down. It's the other one who's married. Raphael Charez. The one who's always in the interview sketches."

"Whew," Dorothy sighed, patting her chest. "Don't do that, Shirley."

"I'm sorry. I heard one of them got married . . ."

"Say, how'd you like to take an ad in our school newspaper, *Weathervane?*" Josephine asked the salesman as Dorothy pulled out her wallet to pay for the posters. "All the Polk kids get it. Look, I have a rate sheet here . . ." She dug into her purse.

"Nah, we don't need an ad," the young man said. "All we get in here's kids."

"Hmmm," Josephine said, looking around. "I see you make up team T-shirts."

"Yeah, that's right . . ."

"Well, my dad coaches a soccer team that both my brothers are on . . . And my mom's on a bowling team at her office . . . Gee . . . that'd sure be a lot of shirts . . . But I guess I'll find a store that wants to take out an ad."

The salesman grunted. "Well . . . Lemme see the rate sheet," he mumbled, and Josephine winked at Shirley while he studied it.

"Ohh—" Dorothy suddenly wailed, "I don't think I've got enough money here for two . . ."

"Well, just get one then," Josephine told her.

"I want two!"

"I'll buy it for you, Dot," Shirley said, opening her purse.

"Oh, Shirl, thanks, I'll pay you back! Will you look at this hunk?" she said, smiling. "Will you just *look* at him?"

3...

Miriam Goobitz frowned as her daughter Rosalyn passed the bowl of mashed potatoes on without taking any.

"You need carbohydrates, Rosalyn," she said, waving a finger. "You need the energy. You want to faint over the counter?"

"I've got carbohydrates all over me, Ma," Rosalyn answered. "You can see them when I stand up. They're all lumped together on my hips and thighs. I'm just a teeming mass of carbohydrates."

20

"I'll eat hers," Annabelle said. "I love mashed pota-toes."

"You could have just a little . . . It wouldn't hurt," Miriam insisted, so with a sigh, Rosalyn dipped a prong of her fork into the bowl.

"You girls see the letter from Susannah?" Leonard Goobitz asked, moving his peas aside with his knife. "She sounds like she's doing fine."

"I didn't see it," Annabelle said, jumping up. "Where is it?"

"Sit," her mother said. "Plenty of time after dinner."

"Well, what did it say?"

"She said they're painting her apartment," Rosalyn said. "Living room and kitchen, white—bedroom, pale blue."

"Uh-huh . . ."

". . . And she went to some club where she saw Ward Price—"

"He's great!" Annabelle cried. "He was a guest host on 'Sound Stage 3' last month. His new record's num-ber eleven on the charts!"

". . . And she got a raise."

"No kidding!"

"Uh-huh. She bought this line of women's suits, or something, and everyone said it was *ug*, you know? No one would be caught dead and all that? Well, Susannah wore one to work one day and now it seems to be the new style in Chicago!"

"Oh, how great!" Annabelle squealed.

"Aren't you proud of your sister?" Miriam said, smil-ing.

"I'm proud of all my daughters," Leonard said. "Please pass the chicken."

"When I was young a woman didn't have such responsibility," Miriam said. "At least not the kind Susannah has. Those were men's jobs. Isn't it nice the way things have changed. So many chances for girls. So, Rosalyn, you going out Saturday night with Robert?"

"No, Ma . . ."

"No?"

"No."

"Such a difference between you and Rebecca. One I could never get to stay home and the other I can't get to leave."

"You want me to leave?" Rosalyn asked.

"Of course not. Just for the evening once in a while. Isn't it funny. One egg, two very different children."

"Uh-uh," Annabelle mumbled, her mouth full.

"What?"

Annabelle swallowed. "Not one egg. That's identical twins. Roz and Bec were two different eggs. Two different sperms fertilized them."

"Such table talk," her father said.

"It's true," Rosalyn said with a smile. "I have a right to be different from Becca. I came from my own egg. Got my own genes." She laughed. "Which are too tight from too many carbohydrates!"

"Different," Annabelle mumbled.

"What?"

"I was just thinking," she answered and got up to clear the table. "Everyone's different. Even people in

22

the same family. Even twins. And each person can make a difference. Look at Susannah. She wore something and because of the way she looked in it, everyone's wearing it. She made a difference all by herself. One person!"

"So?" Rosalyn said. "What about it?"

"It's just the point I've been trying to make with everyone—with my friends, the newspaper, in class—but most people don't seem to want to make a difference. They just want to go along with what already is. We read this story in school—about a boy named Grady something. And he was all upset because of the pollution and litter and stuff in his town. And one day he went on his own campaign to clean up the town, writing letters and picking up trash and everything—and someone got him on TV, and after that the people in the town started caring, too. They got more trash baskets on the sidewalks and swept the streets, picked up after their pets . . . And all because of one kid."

"You want to get on TV, Annabelle?" Rosalyn asked.

Annabelle turned red. "Oh, you sound like Jo," she muttered.

"But what is it you want to do?" her sister asked. "Exactly what?"

"I don't know yet . . . Just something. Something special."

"I think you have a recognition thing," Rosalyn said.

"Don't *you* want to do something?" Annabelle asked her.

"Yes," Rosalyn said emphatically, getting up from the

table. "After we do the dishes, I absolutely want to wash my hair."

Saturday night Helaine had a slumber party. Helaine usually had the slumber parties because she lived in the biggest apartment. Actually, Josephine had the biggest apartment, but she also had the biggest family. Besides her parents and two younger brothers, her immediate household also consisted of an aunt and a cousin.

Helaine's parents didn't mind hosting the party, since everyone chipped in for pizza and Helaine ate her usual salad and ounce of whatever meat was allowed on her diet.

"Too bad Jo couldn't come," Shirley said, breaking a string of mozzarella cheese with her fingers.

"No, she's lucky," Annabelle said. "To go to a fraternity party at City College? That'd be fun."

"But she's going with her cousin. He's no fun. He's a creep," Dorothy said. "Anyway, it's not a party, it's a show. They're putting on a show. Jo's cousin wouldn't take her to a party. Not at the college. She's only a kid."

"Well, I think it sounds like fun, anyhow," Annabelle said. "Did you order anchovies, Dot? Yechh!"

"Give me that piece. You take the half with the mushrooms. Anyway, Jo'll probably miss 'Sound Stage 3' tonight. I don't think that's so lucky. Any date I have has got to bring me home by eleven-thirty or I don't go."

"Oh, you're a real swinger, Dorothy," Helaine said

24

and giggled. "And *please* just eat the pizza and don't talk about it or pass it right in front of my nose."

"You really have willpower," Annabelle told Helaine. "My sister Rosalyn's like that, too."

"Oh, please, if I looked like your sister Rosalyn I wouldn't need willpower. She's like a rail."

"She doesn't think so."

"What time is it?" Dorothy asked.

"Eight o'clock, Dottie," Helaine said. "You have three and a half more hours. Do you want to start counting down now?"

"Don't tease her," Annabelle said. "She's in love."

They played Monopoly and charades and watched television. They experimented with eye shadow, mascara, penciled beauty marks and blusher. They exclaimed over each other's nightgowns and pajamas. They made anonymous phone calls to the captain of the basketball team and to someone named Albert Wzniewskevski whom they found in the phone book. In short, they did everything they usually did when they got together on Saturday nights. Until eleven-thirty. Then they all quieted down.

"Here it comes!"

"Dorothy, you're shaking."

"No I'm not, no I'm not, *sh!*"

And then they were all giggling, chortling, nudging each other.

RAPHAEL CHAREZ (*as a reporter*): Senator, your absence from the floor for that debate about the energy bill was certainly noticeable—

HAP RHYSBECK (*as the senator*): Son, I was researching that bill.

RAPHAEL: Senator, you were on a Caribbean cruise.

HAP: I was researching solar energy, son. Solar energy. It's the wave of the future.

RAPHAEL: But what about the crucial vote on social security, Senator? You know, many old people can't make it today. They're eating dog food. Cat food. They're barely existing, Senator. Now, during the roll call, you were seen at Maximillian's Restaurant.

HAP: I don't deny that I was there, son, but on that day, I *took an old person to lunch!*

" 'Took an old person to lunch!' " Annabelle repeated and slapped Helaine's leg.

"Who's he supposed to be? Which senator?" Helaine asked.

"Oh, you know, the one who missed every vote his whole term. What's-his-name. He just got reelected."

"Oh, him. Yeah."

"*Sh!*" Dorothy said.

In her seat at City College's Little Theater, Josephine stifled a yawn. She looked over at her cousin Fred but he hadn't noticed. His eyes were glued to the stage.

Boy, this is boring, Josephine thought. But Fred sure loves it. At least, he looks like he does . . .

Fred's father, Josephine's Uncle Tony, had been

stricken with a heart attack while lifting four-year-old Fred high over his shoulders so the boy could get a better view of the Thanksgiving Day parade. Uncle Tony had died later that day in the hospital and that very night, Fred and his mother came to stay at the Scarangillos' for a while until they recovered from the shock.

"It's the least I can do for my brother's family," Josephine's father had said. "The least."

"Of course," Josephine's mother had said. "I wish Ramona spoke English."

"I'll speak to her. She can help you with the baby"— meaning Josephine, who was six months old at the time.

It was hard to tell if Aunt Ramona had recovered from the shock because she still didn't speak English, but she and Fred were still at the Scarangillos' fourteen years later. Aunt Ramona had helped raise Josephine and her younger brothers, John and Sebastian.

The only change was that Josephine's mother, a Jewish girl from Tom's River, New Jersey, had learned to speak fluent Italian.

Josephine jumped. She had dozed and now everyone around her was applauding. She began to clap, too, trying to make hers sound as enthusiastic as Fred's.

"Hey, wasn't that great?" Fred asked, turning to her.

"Uh-huh . . ."

"What's the matter with you? I thought it was great."

"Oh, I liked it. I really did, Fred."

"Yeah, but you're not—you know—doing a jig about it or anything . . ."

"No, it was . . . good. The acting was good . . ."

"Darn right. These kids are all going to be stars someday, you watch. They really put soul into this. Oh, look—the composer's taking a bow." Fred stood up and clapped loudly.

"Do you know him?" Josephine asked.

"Sort of. Richie's the one I know best. He played Apollo."

"Oh." Josephine looked at the mimeographed sheet that served as a program. "Apollo? I don't see any Apollo . . ."

"Well, his name was Lance in the play. But it's based on the Daphne myth. Didn't you get that?"

"Uh, no."

"Well, it is. Daphne was this independent chick who knew what happened when mortals were loved by gods. They all ate it. So when Apollo chased her, she got herself turned into a laurel tree. Didn't you catch that reference? Look, they mention it right at the top of the program . . ." He pointed to it on her sheet.

"Must've missed that," Josephine mumbled.

"It was an allegory, Jo," Fred said disgustedly. "If you didn't get all the symbolism, then you missed the whole point!"

"I thought it was supposed to be a revue," Josephine said.

"I never said it was a revue," Fred told her. "I said it was a musical. C'mon, let's go backstage and say hello to Richie and the others."

"Okay . . ." They stood up. "The girl lead was supposed to turn into a tree at the end?"

28

"Uh-huh."

"Well, but in the end she got a job as a photographer's model."

"Right! Get the symbolism?"

Josephine sighed and followed him down the aisle.

"Sorry, Jo," Fred said over his shoulder. "I keep forgetting you're only in junior high."

Josephine rolled her eyes and trudged along behind him.

It was crowded and noisy backstage. Actors in makeup were kissing friends and relatives; college kids in jeans and overalls were walking past them carrying pieces of scenery; food and drinks were being passed from hand to hand.

"Richie!" Fred cried and, grabbing Josephine's wrist, yanked her toward a short boy in a leotard. "Hey, Rich, you were terrific!" Fred said and clapped the boy on the shoulder.

"Thanks, Fred . . ."

"This is my cousin, Jo Scarangillo. She loved it!"

"I loved it," Josephine said.

"Oh, good. Did you like my love song? In the fourth act? 'In a Forest of Lights Sleeps My Love'?"

"Gorgeous," Fred said.

Josephine nodded and said, "Nice."

"There's my mother," Richie said. "Thanks for coming, Fred. Nice to meet you, uh," he said to Josephine, and disappeared into the crowd.

"Great guy, isn't he?" Fred asked.

Josephine nodded and said, "Great."

29

"Think about City when you're thinking college," Fred told her as they rode the subway home. "It's a terrific place, Jo. They're not afraid to experiment there. I'm glad I didn't go to some small college in the boonies somewhere."

Josephine didn't remind Fred that he'd had several rejections from some small colleges in the boonies somewhere. Instead she said, "Well, thanks a lot for taking me, Fred."

"It's okay," he answered. "Mary Sue had to study tonight, anyway."

Oh, boy, Josephine thought. And for this I missed a slumber party and "Live From Sound Stage 3"!

4...

Mr. Hedley smiled at his *Weathervane* staff as he leaned toward them over his desk.

"I know," he began, "that Sammy, here, has spoken to you about drumming up some new ideas for articles, perhaps even a series. Now, we're always trying to improve our paper as well as learn as much as we can about the field of journalism, but now we have even more of an incentive in working toward these goals. Sammy will tell you about it. Sam?" He stepped away from his desk and Sammy Prysock took his place.

"I'm putting this up on the bulletin board right after

the meeting," Sammy said, holding a piece of paper. "It's an announcement about a newspaper contest. For junior high schools in the tristate area. The paper judged to be the best gets a financial award and the writers of the best articles get to be reprinted in some of the city dailies. And it'll probably be on the television news, too, when the contest is over. Now, we want the whole school to know about it so anyone will be able to contribute. But we wanted the staffers to hear about it first." He waved the paper, then put it down. "Any comments? Or questions?"

"Is it any more specific?" Annabelle asked. "Do they say the types of things they want?"

"Well, they break it down . . . There'll be a prize for best layout, photography, things like that. But the most important things are the articles and the ways the reporters get their information."

"Investigative reporting!" Annabelle cried.

"That's me!" Vic DeMarr cried.

"Oh, Vic, you've only done sports," Sylvia Goldberg said. "What've you ever investigated?"

"We've never really done anything like that," Sammy said, looking at the paper's advisor. "Have we, Mr. Hedley?"

"Not to any great degree. It sounds like fun, though. And a good learning experience. If any of you are thinking of a career in journalism, here's a good way to begin it."

"The issue coming up'll be our practice issue," Sammy said, "and the one after that will be the one we submit.

The judges are publishers, editors and reporters, so keep that in mind. We've got a lot of work to do."

When the meeting was over, the five friends went to Annabelle's.

"This is it, girls," she announced. "This is our chance. Up to now it's been peanuts."

Josephine sighed.

"What'll we do, Annabelle?" Shirley asked. "I'll take notes. I brought a steno pad."

"That's why we're meeting. To decide what to do. We'll pick something to investigate and then we'll go out and investigate it."

"But I'm happy selling ads," Josephine said. "I'm good at it. Aren't I, Shirley?"

"Terrific," Shirley agreed.

"I'm not so sure about investigative reporting. You do it, Annabelle."

"No, we all have to do it. Together. The Adam's Ribbers."

"A team," Helaine added.

"Besides, all those investigative reporters have people working for them. They don't do all the digging by themselves."

"Working *for* them?" Dorothy asked with raised eyebrows.

"Oh, you know what I mean. There's research and there're people who cover for you while you sneak into places . . . Things like that."

"You've been watching too much television, Annabelle," Josephine said.

"A big exposé," Annabelle said, a dreamy look on her face. "Think of something we can expose."

"A dope ring," Helaine offered.

"What dope ring?"

"I don't know. Isn't that what they're always exposing?"

"How about corruption in government?" Annabelle suggested.

"What government?"

"Pick one!"

"Annabelle . . ."

"I'm only trying to think big."

"Too much television, Annabelle," Josephine repeated. "I think we have to think a little smaller. Closer to home."

"Television . . ." Dorothy muttered. "Television!"

"What about it?" Shirley asked, pencil poised.

"Closer to home!" Dorothy cried.

"She's delirious," Helaine said.

"No, no, listen. Where do they do 'Live From Sound Stage 3'?"

"Where? I think somewhere down on Second Avenue," Shirley said. "Where the station has its studios."

"Yeah. Sound Stage Number Three," Helaine added. "Why?"

"Because that's an easy place to get to. And we could do an interview with . . . with . . ."

"Don't say it—"

34

"Hap Rhysbeck!"

"She said it."

"Well, why not?" Dorothy cried. "It's perfect. We'll have to be real ingenious about how we get to him. Because it won't be easy. And that's where the investigating comes in. And then we'll write it up so well—showing the influence he has on kids and why and all that—and that'll be the good reporting. Look, the idea has everything we need!"

"Everything *you* need," Annabelle said. "You just want to meet Hap Rhysbeck."

"And *you* want to be famous," Dorothy shot back.

"And how about Shirley and Helaine and me?" Josephine asked. "What do *we* get?"

"To meet Hap Rhysbeck and be famous?" Dorothy said.

"We can have fun," Helaine said. "Sounds like fun."

"Yeah," Shirley said, smiling. "It does."

"But—but—a TV star?" Annabelle protested. "That's not . . . It's not *worthy* enough. I mean . . . those judges will be looking for something . . . *meaningful*. Uplifting. Educational. Something that can make a difference in . . . in the human condition."

"No, wait a minute," Josephine said. "Hap Rhysbeck has sure made a difference in this human's condition . . ." She held up Dorothy's hand. "And in a lot of kids' lives. There's something he gives people—you know that, Annabelle. It's more than just being funny. He speaks to kids. The way our parents and our teachers don't . . ."

"That's true," Helaine said.

Shirley said, "Yeah . . ."

"So if we do get an up-front interview with him . . . we can talk about that. That'll be meaningful enough for kids. And after all, *Weathervane is* a kids' paper."

Annabelle squinted her eyes.

"Besides," Dorothy said, anxious to push Josephine's point while she had the chance, "getting in to see him won't be easy. It'll take guts. And imagination. And that'll be part of the article, too. Oh, come on, doesn't it sound great? Doesn't it? Don't you want to do it?"

"Here's a place to put all that energy you were talking about, Annabelle," Helaine said. "What about it? Money where your mouth is and all that?"

Annabelle looked from one to the other.

"I just sort of had a different idea for an outlet, that's all," she said lamely. "Do you all want to? I mean, Hap Rhysbeck? Really?"

"Yes!" Dorothy cried, clapping her hands.

"Yes," Josephine said with a brisk nod.

"Oh, sure," Helaine said and grinned.

Shirley shrugged. "Yeah," she said.

Annabelle shook her head back and forth. "This wasn't exactly what I had in mind . . ." she said.

"Life does that to you," Josephine said, touching Annabelle's hand. "It rarely gives you what you had in mind. You have to grab the opportunity it does present."

"Sage," Helaine said, nodding. "Very sage."

"Knock it off!" Annabelle cried, laughing, and threw a pillow at them.

36

They all jumped on her, hitting her with pillows from her couch.

"Okay?" Dorothy cried. "Okay? Agreed? We won't stop till you give in!"

Giggling, Annabelle managed to push them off. "Stop it, stop it! Okay, I give up!"

"Yay!" Dorothy yelled.

"I'll think about it," Annabelle said.

Mr. Hedley okayed their project the next day, and they all went right to Helaine's after school.

"You were really impressive, Jo," Dorothy said. "I think Mr. Hedley really liked the idea."

"You were, too."

"Well, my heart was really in it."

"I'm happy for both of you," Annabelle said. "Now what?"

"Well, Mr. Hedley said we should keep a diary," Shirley said, "of everything we do. To show how we track our story. He said that would be interesting. I'll get my steno pad."

"Yeah, but we don't have anything to write yet, Shirley," Annabelle said. "I mean, *just what do we do now?*"

Dorothy took charge. "Get the phone book, Helaine. Look up the network's number and we'll find out the exact address of Sound Stage Number Three. That's the first thing."

"Right," Helaine said and ran for the phone book, glad to have something to contribute.

"All right," she said, after she'd called. "It's eleven-oh-four Second Avenue. That's down around St. Vincent Place. I used to go to ballet school near there."

"You were a ballerina?" Josephine blurted.

"Knock it off, Josephine," Helaine warned.

"I didn't mean anything, I didn't mean anything."

"I can still do it. Fat people can be very graceful, you know."

"I *really* didn't mean anything."

"Okay . . ."

"Besides, you're not fat, Helaine. You're just plump. And you're very cute."

"All *right*, Jo . . ."

"I'm *sorry*, Helaine!"

"*Okay!*"

"Are we finished?" Dorothy asked. "Because if we're all through our sensitivity number, then I think what we should do first is call."

"Call whom?" Annabelle asked.

"Call the studio, Sound Stage Number Three, tell them who we are and what we want."

"That's a good idea," Shirley said. "And it's easy."

"That's the craziest thing I ever heard," Josephine said. "Do you honestly think they'll pay any attention to that kind of phone call? They probably get three thousand of them every minute of the day. No one'll listen to that. Forget it."

"I know that, Jo," Dorothy said. "Don't you think I know that? But it's the most straightforward way and it's worth a try. The worst thing that can happen is they'll hang up on us. Then we'll go for Plan B. But

38

would it hurt to just try this first? We have absolutely nothing to lose."

Josephine shrugged. "Go ahead. Waste Helaine's phone budget. Make the call."

"Okay," Dorothy said. "Well?"

"Well, what?"

"Well, who makes the call?"

"Dottie, you were the one who wanted to call in the first place. You do it."

"No, no, I can't. I'm scared."

"Well, I'm not doing it," Josephine said. "I'd feel like a fool."

"Don't even look at me," Helaine said.

Shirley shook her head.

"I thought you'd never ask," Annabelle said, taking the receiver off the hook. "Read me the number." Helaine read it and Annabelle dialed.

"WCBC, Consolidated Broadcasting Company," the switchboard operator sang in Annabelle's ear.

"Good afternoon," Annabelle said. "I'd like to talk with—"

"Yes?"

"Uh—"

"Hello?"

Annabelle hung up.

"That was great, Annabelle," Josephine shrieked and applauded.

"Annabelle Goobitz, what was that all about?" Dorothy asked.

"I didn't know whom to ask for," Annabelle said. Her

face was crimson. "Let's decide whom we're supposed to talk to, shall we?"

"Right, right. Uh—"

"That's what *I* said," Annabelle muttered.

"Why not just ask for him?" Shirley offered.

"Who?"

"Hap Rhysbeck. Isn't he the one we want?"

"Oh, Shirl! We'd never get him. Don't be silly!" Josephine cried.

"Well, *who*, then?"

"I don't know!"

"Look," Helaine said. "Ask for him. Ask for Hap. The switchboard operator'll probably say we can't talk to him, but we *can* talk to—whoever. You know, the one who takes the calls that come in for stars."

The others shrugged. "Okay," Annabelle said. "I'll ask for Hap. *What if I get him?*"

Dorothy clapped her hands to her mouth. "I'd die," she breathed. "Right here on Helaine's floor. Coronary arrest. I'd be dead."

"Don't worry, Dottie," Josephine said, "We won't get him. You're doomed to live another day."

Annabelle dialed CBC again while Dorothy hugged herself and tried to keep her teeth from chattering.

"WCBC, Consolidated Broadc—"

"Yes, thank you, Hap Rhysbeck, please," Annabelle said, interrupting.

"Who?"

"Hap—Rhys-beck," Annabelle repeated. "He's one of your stars."

"I know who he is, madam," the switchboard operator said. "But he doesn't usually take calls from the switchboard from fans."

"Well, I'm not a fan, I'm a reporter. And that's okay if you can't connect me with him directly. I'll talk to the person who takes his calls. Who is that?"

She could hear the operator sigh.

"Look, honey, why don't you just write him a letter?" she said.

"Please don't call me 'honey,' " Annabelle sniffed. "And I really am a reporter. I want to request an interview with him. This is legit. Honest."

Another heavy sigh from the operator.

"Okay. He's got an agent who deals with interviews. The network has a promotion department that deals with interviews. I suggest you write a letter to our promotion department. Or you could write to Sound Stage's producer, Clay Ellenbogen."

"Well, but that would take too long," Annabelle complained.

"Probably months," the operator said, "just for them to read it. And then assuming you got past the publicity people, the agent and the producer, Mr. Rhysbeck would probably turn you down because, between the rehearsals, the show, the record albums, the personal appearances and the club acts, he's just –too—busy."

Annabelle held the phone away from her ear.

"What happened?" Shirley asked.

"She hung up," Annabelle answered.

"Told you," Josephine said.

"I wonder if she gets paid to be snotty," Annabelle grumbled.

"She probably gets three thousand—"

"I know, 'calls like that every minute.' Still, she ought to be nicer about it."

"Well, we tried the straight way. Now what?" Helaine said.

Josephine bit her lip. "Wait a minute," she said, "I may have an idea."

"What?" four girls cried.

"Remember that show I went to last Saturday night at City?"

"With your cousin Fred?"

"Yeah. Well, those drama majors, they know everything that's going on in show business in the city. I'd bet anything they know a lot more than we do. About when 'Live From Sound Stage 3' rehearses and where the stars hang out . . . All that stuff. A lot of those kids've been on TV themselves, they're real professionals."

"Do you know any of them?" Helaine asked. "Did you meet any last weekend?"

"Well, Fred took me backstage to congratulate some of them after the show . . . I did meet a few people . . . But Fred is the one who really knows them. I'll ask Fred tonight when he gets home. At least it's a start."

5...

Vic DeMarr stopped Helaine and Shirley at the door of the school the next morning.

"Hey, we heard about what you girls are doing," he said with a smile. "You got about as much chance of interviewing Hap Rhysbeck as I have of playing for the Globe Trotters," he sneered.

"Thanks for all the encouraging words, Vic," Helaine said, pushing past him into the hall.

"Yeah," Shirley said.

"I think it's the dumbest thing I ever heard," Vic said,

following her. "Can't believe even someone like ol' Headless gave you the okay on it."

"Well, he did."

"You're crazy, you know?"

"Just for that, Vic, we won't let you come along and meet him when we get the interview," Helaine said over her shoulder.

Vic stopped walking. "Meet him, huh?" he called. Then he frowned. "Yeah, well—I don't think you'll get near him—"

Helaine didn't turn around.

"—But—but it takes, guts, Jacoby!" he called louder. "I mean—you girls got guts!"

Helaine elbowed Shirley as they walked.

"Hear that, Shirl? We got guts."

"Yeah," Shirley said, smiling.

"We heard you're actually interviewing Hap Rhysbeck for *Weathervane!*" Sylvia Goldberg gushed to Josephine and Dorothy at lunch. "That's absolutely fantastic! What a super idea for the contest issue! When does the great event take place?"

"Oh!" Josephine said and looked at Dorothy. "Uh—"

"Pretty soon," Dorothy said.

"Pretty soon? Don't you have a date?"

"We're working on it," Josephine answered. "A friend of my cousin Fred is setting it up. We'll probably know tonight."

"Well, I just want you to know, the whole school is

going bonkers over it. Coolidge is already crazy-jealous, and Colby, too. *They're* working on *old* stuff like the effect of divorce on kids and dope-using, things like that. No one thought of anything this neat! Keep us all posted, okay, Jo? So we can feel like we're all part of it."

"Sure we will, Syl." And after Sylvia had left she added: "Sure, we will . . ."

On the Trail of a Story and a Star

JOURNAL ENTRY 1:
Tried the direct approach. Called the CBC network. Response was totally negative. Operator nasty. Put us off. Reporter J suggested using connection from City College Drama Department. Will follow through tonight.

JOURNAL ENTRY 2:
Reporter J's cousin Fred gave us name and number: Richie Raskin. College student who once auditioned for "Live From Sound Stage 3." Calling R.R. Thursday evening.

Dorothy nudged closer to Josephine, who was holding the phone.

"What's he saying, what's he saying?" she was whispering.

"Sh!" Josephine clapped a palm over the ear that wasn't pressed against the receiver. "What? . . . No, my friend was talking. Say that again. Where? Quick, get a pencil, Dot. Where did you say? Side door next to bakery. No markings. You're *sure* about the time? Well, listen, thanks a lot! No, of course I'll never mention you. I swear! I forgot your name already! I promise, no matter what, no one will ever know you told us." She hung up.

"He said they write and rehearse every day. All week. And the way the cast gets in is through a side door in an alley on the Eighteenth Street side of the building. There are no markings on the door, but it's like a rusty-iron color and it's right next to a bakery. See, the fans all hang around under the marquee in the front, the one that says Sound Stage Number Three, on Second Avenue. Only the 'in' people know about the side door." She smiled at everyone.

"That was good work, Jo," Shirley said.

"Great work," Dot agreed.

"We can go down there right after school tomorrow," Annabelle said. "Now let's figure out exactly what we'll say when we get there."

"How about who we are and what we're doing there?" Helaine suggested.

They all looked at her.

"We learned how well the straight approach works, Helaine," Josephine said. "We have to be devious."

"How about this?" Annabelle said. "We go in this rusty door, right?"

"What if it's locked?" Dorothy wanted to know.

"It won't be locked, people have to come in and go out all the time."

"They probably have their own keys, Annabelle," Josephine said. "I mean, who leaves *any* door unlocked these days?"

"All right . . . First we try to get in. If the door's locked, we knock . . ."

"We knock," Shirley repeated and wrote it down.

"And we say?"

"And we say . . . we have an urgent message for Hap Rhysbeck."

"Who from?" Helaine asked.

"From . . . his mother?"

"Oh, Annabelle!"

"Sister?"

"We don't even know if he's got a sister."

"How about his *broker?*" Josephine suggested.

Annabelle held up a hand. "Just a very—personal—message. We can't say whom it's from."

"Well . . ." Josephine said skeptically. "People probably use that one all the time. Three thousand every minute, I'll bet."

"Well, how about a package?" Annabelle said. "A present!"

"What kind of present?"

"I know!" Annabelle cried. "I'll get Rosalyn to make up one of our special gift packages. A "Good Bits" box. With cheeses and wrapped meats and special pickles. You know the pretty packages we make?"

"Do I . . ." Helaine moaned.

"And it's all covered in that crinkly yellow cellophane so you can see through it? Well, we'll grab it from the deli right after school and take it down there. Special delivery. When they see that package they'll all drool. They've got to let us deliver it."

"That sounds good, Annabelle," Josephine conceded. "Very good. But what if they only let one person in?"

"We *all* have to go in," Dot wailed.

"We'll *all* go in," Annabelle promised. "But . . . if they only let one person in, we'll still be able to get a story . . . Which we wouldn't if they let *no* persons in . . ."

"We all go, Annabelle," Josephine said, closing the subject.

JOURNAL ENTRY 3:
We raced over to Goobitz's after school, where Rosalyn had an absolutely mouthwatering package of Good Bits in cellophane waiting for us. Rosalyn had even put a white carnation on the top of the package. It was irresistible. Reporter H's stomach growled all the way downtown. We had no trouble finding the side door in the alley.

"I'd know it anywhere," Helaine said, "by the bakery smells. Mmmmmph . . ."

"This whole afternoon's been hard on you, Helaine," Shirley said. "First the deli stuff, now the bakery . . ."

"And on top of that, I'm skipping Weight Watchers this week to be with you all. And I'm not sneaking under that cellophane and I'm not rushing into the bakery. I must have a will of iron. I deserve a medal."

Her four friends cheered and applauded and several people on the street turned around.

"Don't clap any more," Annabelle said quickly. "People will think there are celebrities around. Okay now. You all ready?"

"Ready," Dorothy breathed. "Oh, I think I'm going to faint. He's in there right this minute. Right past that door."

"Don't faint! Put your head between your legs quick."

"No, I'm all right . . ."

"Well, let's go. Should we knock or just try the door?"

"Try the door," Josephine said. "Don't knock. We belong here."

"Okay."

"Okay."

"*OKAY*, so who's going to try it?"

"Oh, I will," Annabelle said. And she did.

"Locked."

The girls groaned.

"We'll have to knock." Annabelle knocked three times. They waited. No one answered.

"Knock again," Dorothy said. "Louder."

Annabelle knocked louder. Four times. They waited. Suddenly there was a sound behind the door.

"A lock's turning. They're coming," Dorothy whispered excitedly. "They're opening the door!"

The door opened just wide enough to reveal a man of about sixty in a blue workshirt, overalls and a New York Yankees baseball cap.

"What is it?" the man asked. He sounded tired.

49

"Uh—" Annabelle said.

"We have—we've got a—" Josephine nudged Annabelle with her elbow, since Annabelle was the one holding the package.

"We have a delivery for Hap Rhysbeck," Annabelle said, finding her voice. She held up the appetizer tray.

"Okay, give it here," the man said, holding out his hands.

Annabelle pulled back. "Well, actually, it's a personal—we've got to deliver it personally," she managed.

"Sorry," the man said, shaking his head. "No one gets in here. Want me to take the package or not?"

The five girls looked at each other.

"No, see—we have to get in. I mean, we have to deliver this personally to Hap—I mean, Mr. Rhysbeck. Those were our instructions. From the deli. See? It's a real present. And it's got to go to him personally. Or we'll probably get fired or something."

"Fired, huh?" the man said. "This deli hires five delivery boys—I mean 'girls' to deliver one package? Sorry, kids. You ain't gettin' in here. There's a rehearsal goin' on. Now, I gotta get back. You want this package sent in to Mr. Rhysbeck or not?"

Tears began to drip down Dorothy's cheeks.

Josephine and Annabelle sighed in frustration.

"I guess we might as well send it," Annabelle said. "I sure don't feel like eating it myself."

"All right, send it," Josephine said. "But put a card in. That way we know he'll get it and maybe he'll remember our names."

50

"Right," Annabelle said. "Who's got paper and pencil?"

"Wait a minute. I've got my pad," Shirley said.

The doorman began to tap his foot.

"What'll I write?"

"Write 'For Hap. From Josephine, Dorothy, Annabelle, Shirley and Helaine. Five reporters who would like an interview.' And leave the name and number of the deli."

Shirley wrote. The doorman rolled his eyes at the graying sky.

"Okay," Shirley said. Annabelle lifted the cellophane and Shirley stuck the note in. The doorman took the whole thing without a word and suddenly the door was slammed in their faces.

"Great," Josephine mumbled. "Just great."

"Some reporters we turned out to be," Helaine said glumly.

"Well, look, we tried," Shirley said. "No one can say we didn't try."

"That's not enough, Shirley. We have to regroup and make a new plan." Annabelle frowned at the sidewalk.

"What? What new plan?"

"Let's go get a soda and we'll discuss it."

JOURNAL ENTRY 3 (continued):
Plan B. We retreated to Howard Johnson's on corner. We all ordered sundaes, Reporter H included, but she mostly cried into hers out of guilt. Reporter A suggested a plan initially be-

51

gun by Reporter D, which was: fainting in front of the stage door. Reporter A figured the doorman would have to take us in.

"No way, Annabelle. He's probably seen that trick about three thousand times every—"

"Well, then, you think of something better, Scarangillo," Annabelle snapped. "I just know that if I were a doorman and somebody fainted on the street, even if I thought she were faking it, I couldn't take the chance. I think it's worth a try. I mean, we're *here*, we've got to do *something!*"

"Can anybody think of something better?" Josephine asked.

Helaine said, "Maybe he'll call us. At the deli. Like the note said in the package."

"Yes," Josephine growled, "and we'll all get to the Emerald City without any trouble from the Wicked Witch of the West."

"Well, I can't think of anything else," Shirley said, spooning up fudge sauce. "Who'll do it?"

"You mean, who'll faint? Dorothy. She's the fainter."

"Oh, no, I can't—"

"You did pretty well before . . ."

"But I meant it then."

"Well, *some*body's got to faint."

"Annabelle?"

"Oh, all right."

They trudged back down the street toward the door.

"Do I have to be lying down?" Annabelle asked. "On the dirty sidewalk?"

"Well, if you faint, you have to fall down, dummy," Josephine told her.

"Why don't we just—you know—be supporting Annabelle. We'll all be holding her when he opens the door," Helaine suggested.

"All right," Josephine said. "Come here, Annabelle. Now, let's get our arms around her . . . Come on, Annabelle, go slack. Not *that* slack—"

"It's okay, we've got her," Shirley said, supporting Annabelle's other side. "You can go as slack as you want, Annabelle . . ."

"Moan a little," Helaine suggested.

"Ohhh," Annabelle moaned.

"A little more . . ."

"*Ohhhhh* . . ."

"That's better."

"Is she sick?" a voice asked.

The girls turned, nearly dropping Annabelle.

"What?" Helaine said.

A man with a briefcase was standing next to them.

"Is your friend sick?" he repeated. "Is she all right? Would you like me to get a policeman or someone?"

"Uh, oh, no—"

"No, thanks—"

"No, she's really fine—"

"She'll be all right—"

"Thank you very much, anyway," Annabelle said, peering up at him.

"You sure? Listen, she doesn't look so good . . . How about we get her into the bakery next door," the man suggested.

"She's absolutely fine," Josephine insisted.

"Yes, she gets these things all the time," Dorothy agreed. "We just hold her up a minute till it passes."

"What's the matter?" a woman with a shopping bag asked, stopping next to them. "The girl sick?"

"She says she's fine," the man answered.

"She don't look so fine . . ."

"I'm *fine*," Annabelle said and stood up.

"See? It always passes," Dorothy said, smiling.

"Maybe you should take her into the bakery and call someone," the woman with the shopping bag said.

"I'm fine. Really." Annabelle shook herself. "See? Standing and everything."

The man and woman shrugged at each other and moved on.

"Who said people in a big city don't care about you?" Annabelle said with a grin. "You know what we should do? We should do a survey of your basic people-on-the-street. I'll pretend to be sick and we can see exactly how many people who pass by actually stop to see if—"

"Anna-belle!"

"What?"

"Another time, Annabelle."

"You want to try this again?"

"Yes, but let's make sure there's no one near us this time."

They waited.

When it seemed safe, Annabelle slumped again, supported by Shirley and Josephine, with Dorothy mopping her forehead with a tissue. Helaine knocked on the door, and to their dismay, the same man opened it.

"What now?"

"It's our friend. Annabelle. She just doubled up."

"Doubled up," the doorman repeated.

"She's sick. Honest," Josephine said. "Please . . . can't we just take her inside to lie down for a minute? Just until she feels a little better? Please?"

The man stared at them.

"My gosh, where's your compassion?" Josephine wailed.

"*Ohhhh*," Annabelle moaned and clutched her stomach. Josephine made a grab for her.

"See? She may be *dying!*"

"She ain't dying," the man sighed.

"*Oooooooh!*" Annabelle cried, wincing and trying to force tears.

"She *is!* Look at her!"

Annabelle moaned again and sagged. Shirley dropped her and she fell to the sidewalk, banging one knee.

"Ow!" Annabelle yelled.

"Forget it, kids," the doorman said. "I can't let you in here. I really can't. If you knew how many people pull this stuff . . . Listen: if your friend is really sick, do us all a favor. Go next door to the bakery. They'll let you call a squad car or an ambulance or something. But lemme alone, okay?"

They looked at him.

"Kids," he muttered and closed the iron door.

6...

Helaine closed her apartment door as quietly as she could and began to tiptoe toward her room.

"Is that you, Lainie?" came a voice from the kitchen.

Helaine stopped in her tracks and held her breath.

"I know it's you, Helaine Jacoby! You come right in here!"

With a sigh, Helaine went back down the hall and stood in the kitchen door.

"Hi, Ma," she said.

"And where were you today, young lady?"

"We're covering a story," Helaine said. "For *Weath-*

ervane. The school newspaper. See, there's a contest for the best—"

"I don't want to hear that," Mrs. Jacoby said, holding up her hand. "It's nice you're working on the paper, but not at the expense of your diet."

Helaine's eyes widened. How did she know about the sundae? she wondered. Do mothers have sonar?

"You're skipping Weight Watchers, aren't you, Helaine?"

"Oh, that," Helaine breathed.

"Oh, that?"

"I mean—I just mean—it's only for a week. Only for a week, Ma. And it's just the meeting. I'm sticking to the diet"—she crossed her fingers behind her back—"and I'm losing weight. Steadily. Honest. When I go back next time they'll all die of jealousy."

Mrs. Jacoby leaned against the sink and frowned.

"Listen, Lainie. Is it for me? Am I pushing you for myself? You're the one complaining since grade school about your weight."

"I know . . ."

"You know. Your father works day and night so his beautiful daughter can have the best of everything."

"I know . . ."

"You know. Your father works day and night so his beautiful daughter can wear the prettiest clothes."

"I know . . ."

"You know. He only wants that his beautiful daughter shouldn't be embarrassed any more by unkind remarks."

"I know . . ."

"You know. He only wants his beautiful daughter to be happy! That's all we want! For you to be happy! Now, Lainie, I love all your friends, they're all wonderful girls. But I don't want you following them and neglecting the things that your father works day and night so you can do and be happy."

"It's only a *week*, Ma . . ."

"You have to be faithful to this, Helaine," her mother said. "Or it won't work. No more missing meetings."

"Okay . . ." Helaine uncrossed her fingers. I will never splurge again, she thought. Oh, God, I have had the last sundae of my life . . .

Mrs. Jacoby walked over and squeezed Helaine's cheeks together.

"Look at that face," she said, squeezing harder. "Look—at—that—face! Such a beauty you could be!"

"Ma—please," Helaine managed through pursed lips.

"Such a beauty," her mother repeated and let her go.

Helaine rubbed her sore cheeks. "When's Daddy coming home?" she asked.

"Do I know? Does he ever tell me? The man works day and night."

Since it was Friday, they planned a consolation slumber party at Josephine's.

No one said much during the early evening. Annabelle had brought some sandwiches from the deli and the girls munched them while Helaine picked at cottage cheese and pears. Afterward, they tried to watch television but gave up finally.

58

"There's nothing on," Dorothy said and turned the set off.

"I don't feel like watching anything anyway," Helaine said. "Does anyone have any leftover roast beef or something?"

"My knee is killing me," Annabelle complained.

"All in the line of duty," Josephine intoned.

"I wouldn't even care if we'd gotten somewhere," Annabelle said, "but all we are is out one platter, worth twenty-nine ninety-five, and I've got pebbles in my knee."

"No, you don't, we cleaned it out," Shirley reminded her.

"But we don't have a *story!*" Annabelle wailed.

"And we didn't meet Hap," Dorothy sighed.

"Well, we'll never get *near* them tomorrow," Josephine said. "That's the day of the show. They'll all be frantic. We'll never get in."

Josephine's cousin Fred came into the big living room and flopped onto an overstuffed chair.

"I see all you little birds are still twittering away," he said cheerfully. "Lead turned up dry, huh?"

"The lead was okay, but we didn't get anywhere," Josephine told him. "It's impossible to get into that studio."

"Josefina, ho appena finito di pulire, non mettere in disordine!" Fred's mother called loudly from her bedroom door.

"We won't mess anything up, Aunt Ramona!" Josephine called back.

"Il cibo è nel frigorifero!" Aunt Ramona yelled.

"We know, we already ate!" Josephine yelled back.

"Jo, if she doesn't speak any English, why don't you answer her in Italian?" Helaine asked.

"Josephine gets stubborn sometimes," Fred said to Helaine. "She gives my mother these little tests to see if she really does understand." Fred smirked at Josephine.

"Well, she didn't say anything back, smarty," Josephine said. "She understood me. You know she did."

"No she didn't," Fred said, still grinning. "She just didn't care what you answered. She just wanted you to know she was here. And that she's keeping an eye on you."

"It's *you* she ought to be keeping an eye on," Josephine said, making a face at Fred.

Annabelle pulled herself up from the floor. "Listen," she said, "if the family feud is over, I think we should get back to business. What we need to do is find out where Hap Rhysbeck lives. It'll be easier to stake out his apartment than to get into the studio. I think that's our only hope."

"That's a good idea," Dorothy said, brightening for the first time since their rebuff at the stage door. "Oh, Annabelle, that's a wonderful idea!"

"Where's your phone book, Jo?" Helaine asked.

"Forget *that*, Helaine. He wouldn't be listed. We'll have to find out his address some other way."

"How?" Shirley asked.

"I don't know. My brain is exhausted. I haven't

thought of anything else since we started this story," Annabelle said. "My schoolwork has gone right down the tubes this week."

"Mmm," Josephine agreed, nodding. "But that is a good idea. About finding out where he lives. Any ideas, Fred?"

Fred chewed a fingernail and thought.

"Nah . . ." He said after a minute, changing five facial expressions from hope to dismay. "But I'm going to a party tonight at Tau Delt. Richie Raskin'll be there. Maybe he knows where the guy lives."

"You think he does?"

"All I can do is ask. Well . . . gotta go change. Don't laugh at me when I come out."

"Why? You wearing a suit or something?"

"Worse. A bear costume. Well, half of it, anyway."

The girls laughed.

"A bear costume? You're kidding!" Dorothy cried.

"Well, it's a costume party . . . You have to go as your favorite animal."

"Your favorite animal is a bear?" Shirley asked.

"No, my favorite animal is Mary Sue McHenry. And *she's* going to be in the other half of the suit." He shrugged. "It was the only animal costume the shop had left to rent. Except a gorilla. And besides—gorillas are only one person suits!" Fred stood up and walked into his room.

"A bear costume. Fraternities are crazy. Sororities aren't like that," Annabelle said. "Look at us. We're trying to do something worthwhile."

"Right," Josephine said and laughed. Even Annabelle smiled.

Suddenly, Annabelle's smile faded. She turned white. Her eyes bulged.

"Annabelle?" Helaine said tentatively.

"Is she all right?" Shirley asked.

"This time she's really sick," Dorothy said, moving to touch Annabelle's forehead.

But Annabelle pushed her hand away. "I've got an idea," she said. "This one is a can't-miss. This one is An Idea."

"What?" the other four chorused.

"What is it?" Dorothy squealed.

"It's Fred. It's *Fred!*"

"Fred?"

"Costume party," Annabelle said, a grin beginning to form.

"*What?*" Helaine yelled.

"Tomorrow. Tomorrow afternoon. Just when everything is probably at its most hectic . . . That's when we show up!"

"*Why?*"

"*Where?*"

"To do *what?*"

"To go on!" Annabelle cried and began to scream with laughter, banging the floor with her palms.

"To go *on?* To go on the *show?*" Josephine cried.

"Television adds eight pounds!" Helaine wailed.

"Annabelle, you're crazy," Dorothy said, shaking her head.

"No, no, listen. We get costumes. We disguise our-

selves in costumes. Really great, honest, authentic, ter-
rific-looking costumes. And we show up at the stage
door and we say, 'We're here for the newspaper sketch,'
or something like that. And we walk right in!"

"You *are* crazy!" Dorothy repeated. But not so loudly.

"What kind of costumes?" Helaine asked, frowning.

"Something that will really disguise who we are. So
that doorman won't recognize us at all. Something that
requires masks, or makeup . . . and padding and—and
everything!"

"That's funny, Annabelle," Jospehine said, her fingers over her mouth. "That's really funny. I mean, it's
so crazy that it's funny. It just might work. I mean, it
just—might—work!"

"*That's* not something he sees about three thousand
times every minute, huh, Jo?" Annabelle said.

"No," she answered quickly. "No, it sure isn't."

"Now! What'll we wear?"

"We could use Fred's bear costume . . ."

"Better than that."

"Clowns?"

"Clowns're good . . . Write down clowns, Shirley.
What else?"

"Um . . . How about babies?"

"Babies?"

"Yeah, babies. With lots of curls and rough and lolli-
pops."

"No!" Helaine said. "Not babies. Not me."

"Okay, no babies."

"I know . . ." Dorothy said. "*I* know what . . ."

"What?"

"Remember Jo's crack today? About the Emerald City?"

"Oh, no, Dot," Josephine said, waving her hand. "We'll never get all that stuff in one day—Cowardly Lion, Scarecrow, pinafore—"

"No, not *them*," Dorothy said. "Munchkins!"

"Munchkins . . ." Annabelle said softly.

"Munchkins . . ." Josephine repeated.

Shirley wrote *Munchkins*.

"Munchkins," Dorothy said, "because we can get all that fast and it'll still look authentic. Just a lot of crazy clothes, like striped knee socks and baggy skirts and all different-colored tops and bows and hats and tons and tons of makeup and wigs and beards and—"

"Yes!" Helaine cried. "I love it! I love that, Dorothy! We show up at Sound Stage Number Three—"

"—at around six o'clock in the evening—"

"—and we're all in fantastic costume—"

"—and we say to the doorman, 'It's us. We're here for the munchkin sketch'!"

"*Mio Dio, un orso in casa mia!*" Aunt Ramona shrieked as Fred strolled back into the room wearing the top half of his bear costume.

"Ta—da!" he cried, but no one turned around.

"Hey!" he called. "I just scared my mother half to death. How about you? You'll have to imagine the other half filled by Mary Sue."

No one looked.

"*Hey!*" Fred called again. "What's the matter with you guys?"

64

Annabelle turned around.

"Oh, hi, Fred," she said.

"That's it? 'Oh, hi, Fred'? No laughs, giggles, jeers or stupid remarks?"

"Go wake up John and Sebastian," Josephine said. "They'll be glad to laugh at you."

"I'm leaving," Fred said. "I can tell you're working on something else and I don't want to hear it."

He put his trench coat on over huge brown clawed paws and left the apartment.

"Now, write, Shirley," Annabelle was saying. "Let's pool everything we have!"

"Let me get into my closet," Josephine said and left the room.

"I've got a lavender peasant blouse and a red striped miniskirt," Dorothy said. "And I have two leotards, purple and black . . ."

"I have about a million scarves," Helaine said. "And my mother has a brown bouffant wig."

Shirley was writing frantically. "I've got patent-leather Mary Janes," she said as she scribbled.

"Oh, Shirl! You do? Mary Jane shoes?"

Shirley looked up and blushed. "Well . . ." she said.

"What *else*, little Shirley?" Annabelle asked.

"Makeup," Shirley answered.

"Stage makeup?"

"Everything," Shirley said.

"Oh, Shirley! These quiet ones, you've got to watch them . . ."

"What are you doing with that stuff, Shirl?" Dorothy

asked. "You never said a word. About makeup or anything."

"Well . . . See, my mother's very shy . . ."

"We know that, Shirley. It runs in the family.
What does your mother's being shy have to do with
makeup?"

"Well, she took this course on how to use it. She
thought it would help . . . bring her out."

"It didn't," Annabelle said.

"Yeah, I know. But we still have all the makeup. I
play with it when I have nothing to do. And the Mary
Janes—there're six pairs."

Helaine laughed loudly. "It's a good thing we're your
best friends, Shirley. Don't ever tell *anyone* else you've
got six pairs of patent leather Mary Jane shoes!"

"Are they black?" Dorothy asked, giggling.

Shirley nodded.

"They're black!" Annabelle screamed and doubled
over.

Josephine, who had come back into the room, her
arms laden with clothes, stood over them.

"You dummies, they're her father's, aren't they,
Shirl?"

Shirley, laughing, nodded. Shirley's father was a
buyer for a chain of shoe stores.

"Oh," Annabelle said, straightening up. "Your father's Mary Janes. That's different."

"Look what I've got," Josephine said, dumping the
clothes on the floor. "We'll pick some stuff from this
pile and tomorrow we'll get the rest from your houses.

66

No sleeping late in the morning, ladies. We've got a lot of work to do!"

They decided to dress at Helaine's because both her parents were going to be out all day.

Three of them used Shirley's father's Mary Jane shoes. Dorothy, Annabelle and Shirley herself wore them over purple-and-white, black-and-red and green-yellow-and-orange knee socks. Josephine and Helaine chose to go as male munchkins. Josephine wore a red tunic over red tights.

"You can't wear red over red like that," Annabelle said, looking her over. "You look like a Christmas bell."

"Here, wear these tights," Dorothy said, handing Josephine a pair of yellow ones. "Then you'll look like a diseased mushroom."

"How do you like my bonnet?" Annabelle asked. "Should I tie the bow in front or on the side?"

"At the side. Should I wear a vest over this blouse?"

"Where's the stocking cap? I can't find the stocking cap!"

"Hey, this blue scarf goes better with your outfit. Give me the red one!"

"You're standing on my crinoline!"

Everyone was talking at once.

"Look! These shoes are pointed, actually *pointed!* Aren't they wonderful?"

"Is this wig tilted or is it supposed to look like this?"

"Sh! Stop!" Helaine said finally. "The neighbors'll be

pounding on the ceiling in a minute! Now let's get the outfits organized quietly, and then Shirley will do our makeup. Where is it, Shirl?"

Shirley nodded toward a hatbox on the floor in the corner of the living room.

"It's all there," she said. "Everything we'll need. Do I look okay?" She was wearing a red sweater with puffed sleeves, a patterned Mexican vest, baggy black knickers, and the striped socks and Mary Janes. On her head sat a Swiss yodeling cap with a feather in it.

"You look great, Shirl," Helaine said, and patted her shoulder. "You're all set. Now. Can you help *me* look like a munchkin?"

Helaine wore a beard they made from the mane of an old stuffed lion. Josephine painted her beard on with eye pencil. They all found or made hats and Dorothy wore Helaine's mother's brown wig with a bright scarf tied around it. And Shirley did all their makeup until they almost didn't recognize each other.

"That doorman'll never know us now!" Annabelle squealed. "Is it time to go?"

"It better be," Helaine said. "This mane itches." She wiggled her jaw.

"Don't wiggle! The glue'll come off!"

Annabelle put her hands on her hips. "And just how are we going to get down there?" she asked. "Subway?"

"We can't take a cab. Can you see a cabdriver picking us up?"

68

"We'd better take the subway. It won't be crowded on a Saturday."

"You mean a public vehicle?" Helaine wailed.

"Well, do you want to *walk?*"

"Walk! It's over thirty blocks!"

"And people will still see us, Helaine. It's a nice sunny day out there . . ."

"Oh, all right, let's take a subway. At least it'll be dark."

They took the subway. Hardly anyone glanced at them.

"That's the city for you," Dorothy sighed.

"I'm scared," Helaine said. "Aren't you nervous?"

"Not yet," Josephine said. "But I will be when we get there. Does anyone's parents know where we are?"

"Just out for the afternoon. As usual," Dorothy said. "My parents are having a dinner party tonight, so they didn't pay much attention to me. I just breezed in this morning and breezed right out."

"Rosalyn asked me what my plans were," Annabelle said, "and I told her I was interviewing Hap Rhysbeck this afternoon."

"You *what?*"

"Oh, she just laughed. Wanted to know how he liked the Good Bits package."

"I wonder how he did like it?" Josephine mused. "He didn't call, did he?"

"Of course he didn't call!"

"Here's the stop!" Dorothy said. "We're here!"

JOURNAL ENTRY 4:

We all dressed as if we were part of a sketch on "Live From Sound Stage 3." We were very confident we'd be able to get in. Reporter A said this was truly investigative reporting, and that it was the confidence that would work for us.

They stood again in front of the iron door.

"Knock, Annabelle," Josephine said. "And this time we just walk right past him. Remember, we're actors now. We're part of the show. Just walk—right—in."

"Okay."

"Okay."

"Okay."

Annabelle took a deep breath, smiled at her friends through cherry-red lips, and banged on the door with her fist.

It opened instantly. The doorman was still wearing his blue workshirt, overalls and New York Yankees baseball cap.

Annabelle spoke right up. "We're here for the munchkin sketch," she said and pushed him aside as she stepped in.

"The what sketch?" the doorman asked, but he was still standing to the side and four other munchkins followed Annabelle in.

"Hey, *what* munchkin sketch?" the doorman called again.

"Just *follow* me," Annabelle muttered over her shoulder, and she continued down a long corridor.

Suddenly, there were lights and a lot of activity. Scenery was being moved. People were yelling. Some were running. Doors slammed. Someone bumped into Annabelle.

"Oh, hi," he said, and turned away yelling. "Hey, George! *George!* These lyrics are wrong! We changed them Thursday, remember? Hey, *George!*"

"Did you *see?*" Annabelle whispered, grabbing Josephine's arm. "That was Pete Sadarovski! Did you *see?* He touched me, right here! He said 'Hi!' "

"I saw," Josephine answered. "But don't stop, keep walking!"

"Hya," a woman said, touching Josephine's shoulder. "Are you guys in the butterfly bit? Because that's rehearsing next. Better hurry up." And she was gone.

" 'The butterfly bit'?" Helaine asked.

"I think we're going *on!*" Dorothy cried.

"Never mind that, where are the dressing rooms?" Josephine asked.

"I think they're over here . . ." Shirley was standing next to a room that had the names of two of the female stars in the center of the door. "Look," Shirley said, and pointed.

"She's right. But where's Hap's?"

"Here! It's here!" Helaine was jumping up and down and pointing. "Hap Rhysbeck! It says so. On the door! Right on the door!"

"I'm fainting," Dorothy said. "I mean it. There's his *dressing room!*"

"Don't faint," Annabelle said. "Don't *faint!* We made it. We did it. Now let's get in there!"

"Hey, you guys, you're on!" someone said, appearing from another room. "Get in there! The butterfly bit is on!"

The girls froze. Hap Rhysbeck's dressing room was to their left. The large studio they were being ushered into was on their right. They looked from one direction to the other. Then all at once, they flew into action.

Annabelle and Dorothy headed for Hap Rhysbeck's dressing room. Josephine and Helaine rushed for the studio door. Shirley, still making up her mind whom to follow, stood in the middle with her arms raised. The unknown woman, trying to grab at Annabelle, bumped into Helaine who knocked against Shirley.

The studio door opened again and a man appeared.

"There's too much noise out here, Marsha," he said.

"Aren't you doing the butterfly bit now, Clay?" Marsha asked.

"Yeah . . ."

"Well, aren't these guys in it?"

The man looked at Helaine and Shirley, sprawled on the floor, at Annabelle, who's hand was poised to knock on Hap Rhysbeck's dressing room door, at Josephine and Dorothy, white under their makeup and staring back at him.

Suddenly, the doorman appeared in the corridor.

"Hey, Mr. Ellenbogen, you doing a munchkin sketch?" he asked.

"A what?"

"A munchkin sketch."

"Not this week . . ."

"Well, who're these guys, then?" He swept his arm around, taking in the five girls. "They said they were here for the munchkin sketch."

The producer, Clay Ellenbogen, said, "Wait a minute . . ." and stuck his head back into the studio. "Ralph! You got everybody there for the butterfly thing? You do? Okay, never mind!" He turned back to the group. "Who are ya?" he growled.

As if on cue, Helaine's mane peeled away from her chin and dropped onto her lap.

"Kids!" the doorman cried.

"Oh, jeez, get 'em outa here, will ya?"

"No, no, we're too close!" Annabelle yelled and pounded on the dressing room door as Helaine and Shirley slowly rose from the floor.

"Come on, you kids," the doorman said. "Mr. Rhysbeck's onstage—he's not in there anyway. Let's go."

7...

"What, no slumber party tonight?" Rosalyn asked Annabelle, who was slumped over the kitchen table.

"No, we had one last night. Besides, we're all tired. We had some day."

"Uh-huh . . . How did your interview go? With Hap Rhysbeck." Rosalyn chuckled.

"Don't laugh," Annabelle said. "We nearly made it. By the way, did you get any calls today? At the deli? We left our card in the Good Bits platter."

"Did we get a call? From Hap Rhysbeck? Oh, sure.

He called to thank us for our generosity and to tell us how marvelous the food was."

"*Really?*"

"Don't be silly."

"Oh."

On Sunday afternoon, the girls met at Annabelle's. The prevailing mood was cloudy, with chance of rain.

"Don't anybody laugh," Josephine said, slouching on the sofa. "The sound would be painful."

"I'm tired," Helaine said. "I slept twelve hours and I'm still tired."

"I couldn't be more depressed," Dorothy said. "I absolutely can't stand it. One minute we're so excited and happy and the next we're all dying. It's too much . . . Life is too much."

Annabelle sighed. "We can't give up, though. The whole school knows we're doing this interview."

"And Coolidge and Colby, too," Shirley reminded them.

"Oh, please . . ." Helaine moaned.

"No," Dorothy agreed, "we're not giving up. But what now?"

"Annabelle suggested we find out where he lives," Josephine recalled. "And I guess that's what we'll have to do now. We can't ever go back to that studio." Her hand flew to her throat. "I'd die of embarrassment if I ever saw that doorman again. Or any of those other people."

"Well, how are we going to find out where he lives? He's not exactly listed in the phone book."

"Right."

"Right."

"Right."

"Annabelle, have you got anything to eat around here?"

"Yes, Helaine, but don't do that."

Helaine made a face. "Okay . . . What should I do, then?"

Josephine said, "We can talk about sweaters for Adam's Ribbers, we can go out and sell some more ads for the paper, we can do our homework, we can listen to records . . ."

"Nah . . ."

"Nah . . ."

"Nah . . ."

There was a collective sigh.

"Did anyone watch 'Sound Stage 3' last night?" Shirley asked.

"I was asleep by nine-thirty," Helaine said.

"Me, too," from Annabelle.

"I saw it," Shirley said. "I wanted to see the butterfly sketch."

"Oh, yeah! How was it?"

"It wasn't too funny. I think they should have used us."

As they all laughed weakly, the phone rang.

"Annabelle? It's me," Leonard Goobitz said. "Listen, your sister has a date."

"Rosalyn? She does?" Annabelle clapped her hand

over the receiver. "Rosalyn has a date," she whispered to the other girls. "Who with, Pop?"

"A nice boy. He's been here all morning, eating salami and eggs. He asked your sister to go to a museum with him this afternoon."

"Is he cute?" Annabelle asked, as her friends gathered around the phone.

"Cute, shmoot," her father said. "He had on a City College sweat shirt, he wears glasses, he's very quiet. Your mother's in heaven."

Annabelle repeated the description to the others.

"He sounds like Fred," Josephine said. "He sounds just like Fred."

"Well," Annabelle said into the phone, "that's nice, Pop. Is that what you called for?"

"No, darling. I called because it's busy here. You better come in and work in your sister's place. I hope I didn't mess up any of your plans."

"No, Pop, of course not. I'll be right over."

"That's my baby," her father said and hung up.

"I have to go," Annabelle said. "But you all stay. And if you think of anything good while I'm gone, leave me a note. Call you when I get back!"

Josephine slammed the door of her apartment and tripped on Sebastian's sneaker.

"Sebastian-get-your-stuff-up-off-the-floor-you-*slob!*" she screeched.

"Eh! *Chiudi la bocca*, Josefina!" Aunt Ramona cried, appearing from the kitchen.

"Sorry, Aunt Ramona . . ."

"Ricordati, la famiglia è tutto," her aunt cautioned as she wiped her hands on her apron and returned to her work.

"Remember, family is everything," Fred called from his room.

Josephine walked to his door. "You're 'everything,' huh, Federico?" she said, and stuck out her tongue at him.

"Aren't we in a cute mood," he said.

"Did you take out Rosalyn Goobitz this afternoon?" Josephine asked, suddenly suspicious.

"Who, me? Are you kidding?"

"Well, you're wearing a City College sweat shirt and you wear glasses . . ." She frowned.

"So? Is that a requirement for taking out the Corned Beef Queen of Sixth Avenue?"

Josephine put her hands on her hips. "You should be so lucky," she said. "Rosalyn is too good for you. Stick to Mary Sue, the Silicone Queen of City College!"

"*You* should be so lucky," Fred laughed. "What's the matter with you, anyhow?"

Josephine went over and sat on his bed.

"We have to get an interview with Hap, Fred. And we just can't find any way to do it. And it's getting very frustrating."

Her cousin shook his head. "Look, Jo—you'll never be able to see the guy. He's the hottest thing in the whole country and you're just kids. Forget it. Write the story of how you tried. It'll be funny and interesting and just as good. Probably better, believe me." He turned back to his desk.

"Yeah . . . Mr. Hedley suggested that. But it's like a bug now. We can't stop. I mean, it'd be different if he were out in Hollywood or something, but he's *here*, just a few blocks away!"

"*Everything's* just a few blocks away, Josephine. And it might as well be on Mars. Forget it, I'm tellin' you. Mama's making canneloni . . . Go have some. *Mangia*, sweetheart. And forget."

"Did you go out with Fred Scarangillo this afternoon?" Annabelle asked Rosalyn when she got home that evening.

"Fred Scarangillo?"

"I didn't think so. Well, who *was* he? And *how* was he?"

"Listen, thanks for working today," Rosalyn said. "I appreciated it. He was nice."

"Just 'nice'?"

Rosalyn shrugged. "Yeah. Real quiet. Except he likes art. He talked about art. In the museum."

"Well, will you see him again?" Annabelle asked.

Rosalyn shrugged again.

"What's his name?"

"Harvey . . ."

"He sounds like a 'Harvey.' "

"Stop it, Annabelle. He really was nice. He loved my eggs."

79

"Well, you had a better time than we did," Annabelle said. "We've got to think of a way to get to Hap Rhysbeck and it has to be soon." She held up a piece of paper. "Shirley left me a note. It says: 'Over to you.' That means they didn't have any ideas while I was down at the deli. Do you think we should send over another Good Bits tray?"

"Not on your life," Rosalyn said. "Not at that price."

"Yeah . . . And not even a thank-you note, either," Annabelle mumbled. "I'm not sure I even like him very much any more."

"Well, then forget about the story," Rosalyn said. "Or pick someone nicer."

"Nope. We're going for this one."

The next day was Monday, the regular meeting day of Adam's Ribbers at Annabelle's house. Everyone showed up except Shirley.

"Where is she?" Dorothy asked, bewildered. "I can't remember ever being without Shirley."

"Me, neither," Josephine said. "Did you see her in school today?"

"Come to think of it, I didn't," Annabelle said, frowning.

"I didn't either," Helaine said. "But Shirley's *always* there."

"Always. Shirley's always there. Shirley's never not there."

"Well, she's not here," Josephine said.

"Give her five minutes, then call. She may show up."

No one waited the five minutes. The Fergusons' phone rang and rang.

"No answer," Annabelle said. "I'm getting worried."

"Call her father."

"At work? Don't be crazy. Besides, he's always on the road or something."

"Well, her mother doesn't work . . . And nobody's home! This isn't like Shirley," Helaine said. "She'd call. She'd let us know if she weren't coming today."

"How do you know? She's always *been* here."

"That's why."

They spent the afternoon dialing Shirley's number and chewing their fingernails.

At six o'clock everyone left and Annabelle's mother came home.

"What's with the long face?" Miriam Goobitz asked as she took off her sweater.

"We don't know where Shirley is," Annabelle told her. "She wasn't here today and we can't get her on the phone."

"Shirley? Shirley Ferguson?"

"Yeah, what other Shirley is there?"

"But she's always here."

"We know . . ."

"Well, I have something nice to tell you—Rosalyn's out!"

"She is? With Herman?"

"Harvey. Such a Harvey. He brought her roses."

"Roses?"

" 'Roses for Rosalyn,' he said. Don't make a face, Annabelle, so he's not Mister Originality. He's nice. When his skin clears up he'll be even good-looking."

"You want me to work tonight, Mom?"

"No, it's an early date. He has to be home to study. They went to a five o'clock movie, they'll come back and eat at the deli, then he'll go. He loves our food."

"Oh, no wonder you love him," Annabelle said with a grin. "Wait till he tastes *my* sandwiches."

"Stay away from him. This one is your *sister's*. And it's about time—"

She stopped as the phone rang. Annabelle raced for it.

"Hello, Annabelle," the voice said, "it's Mrs. Ferguson . . ."

Annabelle's heart sank.

"Did Shirley stay late at your house, Annabelle? I'm getting worried . . . It's almost six-thirty. My aerobics class was cancelled, so I came home early. But Shirley should have been here by now . . ."

Annabelle said, "Uh—"

"I know she's always there on Monday afternoons, right?"

"Always," Annabelle said.

"So when did she leave?"

Annabelle looked at the ceiling. Then at her mother. Then at a lamp.

"Annabelle?"

"Mrs. Ferguson . . ."

"Yes?"

"Mrs. Ferguson . . ."

"What *is* it, Annabelle?"

Annabelle's mind raced. Okay, she decided, this is no time for misplaced loyalty. Jo, Dorothy, even Helaine—they might have skipped off somewhere and not mentioned it at home. But Shirley? Our Shirley? Oh, no, something's happened to Shirley . . .

"Mrs. Ferguson," Annabelle said, "Shirley wasn't here today and we've been kind of worried about her because we couldn't reach her at home—"

"She wasn't *there?*"

"No . . ."

"But she's *always* there!"

"I know . . ."

"Did she say anything in school today?"

"Mrs. Ferguson—we didn't *see* Shirley in school today . . ."

"Oh, my God—"

"Please don't worry," Annabelle said as she felt a trickle of perspiration behind her ear. "Kids do this all the time . . . I'm sure she had something important to do . . ."

"*What?*"

"I don't know."

"I'm calling the police, Annabelle. If you hear anything, call me immediately."

"I will . . ." Annabelle hung up. "Mrs. Ferguson's calling the police," she told her mother.

"Oh, my God—"

"I'm sure she's all right," Annabelle said.

The phone rang.

"Annabelle?"

"Dottie! Shirley's not home. Her mother's calling the police."

"I know. I just tried her again and her mother told me to get off the line. Where could she be?"

"I don't know. Think. Where would she go?"

"I don't *know!* She's always *around!*"

"I know, I know . . ."

"Oh, Annabelle, I'm scared."

"I'm not. She's all right."

"You're not scared?"

"No," Annabelle said. The receiver shook in her hand.

"If you hear anything, call me right back."

"You, too."

As soon as she hung up, the phone rang again. It was Helaine.

"Shirley's line is busy, your line was busy, Dot's line was busy. What's happening?"

Annabelle told her. "Call Jo," she said, "and tell her. Maybe she can think of something."

Annabelle's mother made her nightly call to check on things at the deli. Then she and Annabelle, clutching hands, sat next to the phone and stared at it.

At ten minutes after seven, the phone rang. Mrs. Goobitz grabbed it first, much to Annabelle's consternation.

"*Shirley?* Shirley Ferguson, is that you?" Joy and relief flooded Mrs. Goobitz's face. Then her expression changed radically. "Shirley Ferguson, do you know what you did to us? Not to mention your poor mother! Shirley Ferguson, what we went through—"

"Ma, she hasn't had a chance to tell you what happened," Annabelle growled at her mother, but Miriam Goobitz was not to be stopped.

"I know you're fourteen years old and in the ninth grade but as far as I'm concerned you're not too old to be spanked, young lady. Shirley Ferguson, I've known you since practically you were a baby, so I'm talking to you like a mother. You should know how worried everyone was and Shirley Ferguson, I never thought of all people you would be the one to get this lecture— maybe my Annabelle, but not you, Shirley Ferguson— here's my daughter!"

Annabelle grabbed the receiver from her red-faced mother, held it tightly for a moment, took a breath and put it to her ear.

"Hello, Shirley Ferguson," Annabelle said softly.

"I'm so sorry, Annabelle," Shirley said.

"Well, you should be, you nut."

"Your mother was right . . . But I didn't mean to worry anyone. My mother was supposed to be gone until about nine tonight, so I didn't think of calling home . . ."

"Well, what about *us?*"

"I don't know . . . I guess I didn't think you'd miss me. Well, not that much anyway—that you'd be worried. Anyway, I kind of wanted to surprise you."

"Well, you did, Shirley . . ."

"No, I don't mean *that* way. Hold on a minute . . ." Shirley put down the phone before Annabelle could say anything.

"Where was she?" Annabelle's mother demanded.

"She didn't say yet."

"All that time and she didn't say yet?"

"No."

"I want to know where she was."

"Well, so do I, Ma—"

Shirley came back on the phone. "I had to give my mother an aspirin. She's lying down. Honestly, I had no idea everyone would be so bananas."

"Did you talk to anyone else? Jo, Helaine?"

"No."

"Well, they're going crazy, too, Shirl, so tell me quick what happened so I can call them."

"Oh, okay! I don't want anyone else to worry any more. Annabelle, I found out where Hap Rhysbeck lives. Bye!" The phone went dead.

Annabelle stared at it.

"What did she *say?*" Miriam Goobitz demanded.

Annabelle stared at the phone.

"And then she hung up? *Why?*" Dorothy screamed.

"So I could call you and the others. So you wouldn't worry any more."

"And she never told you what happened."

"She told me she found out where Hap Rhysbeck lives."

"Call Helaine and Jo. I'm picking you up. We're going over there!"

8...

"Well . . ." Shirley said, her bunny-slippered feet curled under her, "I never have missed school before, at least in the last four years, so I decided I could take just one day off . . ."

"Is this the beginning, Shirley?" Josephine demanded. "Because I want you to start from the beginning."

"It *is* the beginning. I went to the library. I figured I'd look up as many back issues of show business newspapers and magazines as I could and maybe I could find

87

out something. And surprise you all. They have all that stuff on microfilm, you know . . ."

The girls looked at each other.

"So I spent the morning reading. All that stuff—*Backstage, Variety*, everything I could get my hands on."

"And?"

"And I didn't find any addresses, but I did read that last June, Hap Rhysbeck had an emergency appendix operation. He was rehearsing some summer stock show and he was rushed to the hospital."

"*So?*"

"So, they said the hospital was St. Michael's."

"*SO?*"

"Well, since that was the only information I had, I went over to St. Michael's to see if I could check some records and find his home address."

Dorothy looked at Annabelle. "I think I'm going to faint," she said.

"I don't b*elieve* this," Helaine said, throwing up her arms.

"I wanted to surprise you," Shirley repeated softly.

"Go on."

"Well, I had lunch—a hot dog from a Sabrett stand—and then I went right to the emergency room."

"They wouldn't tell you anything, Shirley," Josephine said. "They probably get three thousand requests for people's home addresses every single minute."

"Well, they did . . ."

"What?"

"It took all afternoon and part of the evening, but I

got it . . ." She waved her steno pad at them. Dorothy made a grab for it. "*Wait*, let me finish. There was this nurse on duty there. Her name's Violet and she's very nice. She said she couldn't show me any records."

"Told you."

"So I said I understood, even though it was almost a matter of life or death in the sense that all our reputations were on the line. And we'd never be able to hold our heads up in school again. I told her about Vic DeMarr and how he'd never let us forget it if we didn't get the story. And about the contest, of course, and about Coolidge Junior and Colby and all the kids who were just waiting for us to fall flat on our faces. Well, she sympathized, but she said she couldn't do it. So I said okay, but could I just stay and talk to her and help her out."

"Yeah . . . ?"

"Well, it was nice . . . She showed me how to change bedpans and how to make a hospital bed and I typed stuff for her and brought her things and calmed people in the emergency waiting room and got coffee and sandwiches from the cafeteria . . ."

"Oh, Shirley . . ."

"And around six o'clock, she was going off duty. And she thanked me for being such a help. And she said there was a record book on her desk and asked me if I wouldn't mind doing one more thing and filing it for her before I left. And I said I'd be glad to. And she left. And I filed it."

"But not before checking it over."

"Right."

Now all three girls screamed together: "*And it was the book with Hap Rhysbeck's address in it!*"

"No, it wasn't. But the one next to it was."

Josephine slumped back. "Shirley Ferguson," she said.

"Shirley Ferguson," Annabelle echoed.

"Weren't you scared?" Helaine asked.

"I wasn't then, but I am now. My mother grounded me and she called my father in Oneonta and he yelled at me and all of you were so worried—I mean, I just didn't think it would be such a big deal. My mother wasn't even supposed to be home!" She looked at the still-stunned faces of her four friends. "I just wanted to surprise you . . ." she said.

JOURNAL ENTRY 5:
Only three of us were available for the stakeout at His Building after school Tuesday. Reporter H was afraid to cut Weight Watchers again and Reporter S was grounded and had a violin lesson anyway. We did not expect Subject to be around anyway during the afternoon, but we wanted to conduct a preliminary casing of the joint just in case.

"Oh, boy, another doorman," Annabelle groaned.

"He probably chases away about three thousand kids every single minute," Josephine said, shaking her head.

"Well, we're the only ones around here that I can see."

"You watch. It'll start to crowd up with kids. I'll bet anything."

"No, it won't, Jo, because no one knows where he lives. Not everyone has a Shirley of their very own, you know."

"I guess that's true." Josephine looked over at Dorothy, who was staring at the modern-looking building with her mouth open. "This is Earth calling Dorothy Susan Pevney, come in, Dorothy . . ."

"This is his building," Dorothy breathed.

"Yeah, now we have to figure a way to get into it," Annabelle said.

"This is his building," Dorothy said again.

"It would help if we knew the floor," Josephine said, frowning.

"A sure way would be for each one of us to take turns sitting here around the clock. That way one of us'd be sure to catch him," Annabelle mumbled, scratching her head.

"Oh, sure, one of us is sure to be able to sit out here at three o'clock in the morning. Besides, we agreed we all have to see him together."

"This is his building," Dorothy said, swaying a little.

"Stand her up, Annabelle. Well, what do you think?"

"Maybe we should get to know someone who lives here and then we could get to go visit them. That way we'd be in the building."

"How do we do that?"

"We nab a dog-walker."

"Oh, that's a good idea. But pick someone with a small dog."

"He lives here," Dorothy sighed.

"Catch her, Jo, she's listing toward you. Do you think the doorman'll get suspicious if we just hang around here till someone starts to go in with a dog?"

"I think we have to get to the person *before* he starts to go inside, or the doorman will overhear our conversation and know we're just trying to get in."

"Mmmm, you're right. Do you want to go to different street corners?"

"Well, we can't go too far away or we won't know if they're heading for this building or not."

"He probably stood on this very ground," Dorothy moaned softly. "Right on this very spot . . ."

"Pull yourself together, Dottie," Josephine said. "We're developing our plans now. We don't want to have to explain everything to you later."

"But do you realize that his shoes and this sidewalk probably made contact right where I am at this very moment? Do you both realize that?"

Josephine put her arm around Dorothy's shoulders.

"You're right, Dorothy," she said. "So think of this as a secret kiss between his shoes, your shoes and the cement. And help us pick out a dog-walker about to go into seven-twenty-four East Sixty-fifth Street."

"That's dumb," Dorothy said.

"What?"

"If you talk to someone going inside, the doorman will hear you."

Josephine looked at Annabelle.

"Well, we thought we'd stroll down the street a bit

and catch them before they get within hearing distance," Annabelle said patiently.

"Yeah, but then how will you know they're going to *this* building?" Dorothy asked.

Annabelle looked at Josephine.

"That's just what we were discussing before you joined us, my dear," she said.

"What we do is, we pick someone coming *out* of the building. Then we *follow* him and talk to him. That way there's no guessing game about it."

Josephine looked at Annabelle.

"Spacey-Dot is right," Josephine said. "Why didn't we think of that? We were here all the time."

"Nobody's perfect," Annabelle said.

"I wish Shirley and Helaine were here," Dorothy said. "Especially Shirley because she was the one who got us here in the first place."

"Right, and that's why she's grounded," Josephine said. "Besides, she's got violin. And I'm taking over for her on the journal notes, so she and Helaine'll get all the details."

"Well, okay," Annabelle said, peering around. "We've been here long enough already. Let's wait across the street and grab the first person who comes out."

"Him?" Dorothy asked.

"No, not him," Annabelle said.

"Why not? He might be just right."

"Because he looks like he's about a hundred and eight

years old, that's why. He looks like he'll die before he gets a chance to go back in, that's why."

"You know, Annabelle, that's a very bigoted remark. Just because he's old doesn't mean he's useless, you know . . ."

"*I* know that. I didn't mean anything except that when you get very old sometimes your hearing starts to go and I don't want to pick someone we'd have to yell at, that's all. We're supposed to be as hush-hush as we can about all this."

"Well, you're too late anyway," Josephine said. "He just got into a cab."

"Wait," Annabelle said. "Someone else will come out. We *do* have time you know."

They waited.

They argued about, and so lost: a little girl and her governess, a harassed-looking man with a briefcase, two middle-aged women wearing hats and a young woman greeting a young man.

"I'm getting tired of this," Josephine complained. "And I'm getting cold, too. This is more than a fall breeze we're standing in, this is a *wind*. Let's pick somebody!"

"You could never be a real reporter, Jo," Annabelle told her. "Or a detective. Or a paparazzi. Sometimes they stake out a joint for hours. Days, even. The person we pick has to be just right. It can't be someone too young or too old. Or someone in a hurry. Or someone who looks like he never met a kid in his whole life. Just look for someone—ah!"

They followed her gaze.

94

A man with a beard, wearing jeans, stepped out of the building with a schnauzer on a leash. He stopped, greeted the doorman, looked at the sky and sniffed the air, smiling.

"That's our man," Annabelle said. She began to walk in his direction, though on the opposite side of the street. Josephine and Dorothy followed.

"How long do we tail him?" Dorothy asked.

"Just till we get far enough away from the building," Annabelle said, walking faster. When they reached the corner, she said, "Okay. Now!"

They all crossed the street. The man had stopped to let his dog sniff a shrub.

"Hello there," Annabelle said.

"Hya."

"That's a cute dog," Annabelle said.

"Mm."

"What's its name?"

"Hermione," the man answered. "What's yours?"

"Annabelle. This is Josephine. And this is Dorothy."

"Girls . . ." He nodded.

"Listen," Annabelle said, deciding that that was enough small talk, "you look like a nice guy . . ."

"Thank you."

"So we were wondering if you could do us a favor."

The man sighed.

"No, this is no big deal," Annabelle continued. "The thing is, we just saw you come out of seven-twenty-four."

"Yeah . . ."

"And we need to get in there."

"Oh, yeah? Why?"

"Oh, you know why. You know who lives in your building."

"Who?"

"Hap Rhysbeck, that's who!"

"Oh, yeah? No kidding?"

"Didn't you know?" Dorothy asked.

The man replied, "Look, it's a big building."

"Well, he does," Annabelle said. "And we need to meet him. Look, we're not just dumb fans . . ."

"Ri-ight," the man said.

"We're *not*. We need to interview him. For our newspaper."

"Su-re," the man said.

"It's true!"

"So what do you want from me?"

"Well, we thought you'd know what floor he lived on . . ."

The man shook his head.

"But maybe you could just get us inside. Then we could find out for ourselves."

"Look," the man said, "it's a big building, as I said. You can't just wander around in it by yourselves. Anyway, I don't even live there. See, I'm just house-sitting for a friend. And taking care of her silly dog."

"Oh," Annabelle said.

"You don't like dogs?" Josephine asked.

"Not ones that wear bows in their hair," he answered and glowered at the schnauzer.

"It's not the dog's fault," Annabelle sniffed. Josephine nudged her with her elbow.

"We'll be glad to walk her for you," she said with a big smile.

The man put his lips together and nodded. "Yeah, I get it. You walk the dog, you get into the building, right?"

Josephine smiled. "We-ll, you scratch our backs, we'll scratch—"

"Look, girls, it's okay with me, but I'm leaving tonight. My friend's ship docks at eight, she'll be here by ten and I'm gone."

"What's your friend's name?" Dorothy asked.

The man smiled.

"Oh, at least tell us her name," Annabelle begged. "Please?"

"*Please*," Dorothy wailed.

"Just don't mention me, okay?"

"Swear!"

The man sighed.

"*Please!*" Josephine yelled and Hermione barked.

"All we'll do is ask to walk the dog," Dorothy said, "and that's all."

"Okay, okay. Her name is Alexandra Whitehead-Lake."

Annabelle said, "You're kidding."

Josephine nudged her. "Just don't tell him *yours*," she whispered.

"Thank you," Dorothy said.

"You're welcome."

• • •

Shirley hung up the phone and scratched her leg with her violin bow.

"Shirley, why aren't you practicing?" her mother called from the living room.

"I was on the phone!"

"I want to hear that violin, Shirley . . ."

Shirley put down the bow.

"Shirley?"

Shirley's lip quivered.

"Well?"

Shirley turned and went to find her mother. Her face was very red.

"What is it, dear?" her mother asked, looking up from her newspaper.

"Mama, the girls went to the apartment I found and they're going dog-walking tomorrow and I want to go with them . . . Please, can't I go, Mama?"

Shirley's mother frowned. "You want to go *dog*-walking?"

"I was the one who found the apartment and now everything's going to happen without me!" She began to cry.

"Now, Shirley, you're grounded because of the scare you gave everybody."

"But you weren't supposed to be home. If you were home, I'd have called!"

"Yes, but you skipped school."

Shirley's tears fell rapidly. "But, Mama, they're all going to meet Hap Rhysbeck, and they'll all be together, and I'll be left out. I wanted to do something important, like Annabelle always says, and I did, and now I don't get to be in on the end of it . . ."

Mrs. Ferguson touched her lips with her forefinger.

"This is the most fun thing we've ever done, Mama . . . And I played a big part in it! It was my first idea, Mama . . . My first real idea."

Her mother said, "Oh, Shirley . . ."

"Oh, Mama, you do understand, don't you!" Shirley cried.

Her mother thought about the course she'd taken in makeup—and the aerobic dancing, to make her more confident, to 'bring herself out.' She sighed.

"Listen, I'll tell you what I'll do, Shirley . . . I'll talk to your father tonight."

"Thanks, Mama!"

". . . You're welcome . . ."

Annabelle heard the click of the latch and looked at her clock-radio. The digital dial glowed 2:10. She turned on her night light and tiptoed out of her room.

A shadow moved in front of the living room window.

"Roz?" Annabelle whispered.

"What are you doing up, Annabelle?"

"I heard you come in. You never stayed out this late before. And on a weeknight . . ."

Rosalyn giggled. Annabelle couldn't remember ever hearing Rosalyn giggle.

"Well, there's a first time for everything," Rosalyn said.

"Harvey again?"

Rosalyn giggled.

Annabelle rolled her eyes and turned on a low lamp. "He must really be something," she said.

"Oh, he is."

"Rosalyn, are you wearing *eye shadow?*"

Rosalyn smiled and batted her lashes at her sister.

Annabelle shook her head in disbelief. "You *can't* be in love after only three days," she said, folding her arms.

"Who says I can't?"

"Are you *really?*"

"Are Mom and Pop sleeping?"

"Yes. Are you going to wake them up?"

"Of course not." Rosalyn sank into the overstuffed chair. "I was afraid they'd have waited up for me or something."

"Naw, they're tired. You should be, too, after working all day. When do I get to meet him?"

"Who, Harvey?"

"Well, who else, Rosalyn?"

"Good—night—Annabelle," Rosalyn sang.

"What do you mean, good night? I asked when I get to meet the love of your life. Mom and Pop have met him, what about me?"

"I don't know," Rosalyn said. "You might intimidate him."

"Oh, brother . . ."

"I want to keep him to myself for a while," Rosalyn said.

"Oh, come on . . ."

100

"You'll meet him, Annabelle, honest. But he's on a weird schedule, so we either go out early or late. Anyway, you're so busy with your newspaper story, you haven't been around."

"Yeah, and we seem to be getting nowhere . . ."

"Oh, well," Rosalyn said, "you're a plugger. If you make up your mind, you'll get it done. Gee, I've got to get some sleep. And you do, too, Annabelle. Go to bed." She disappeared into her room.

"Thanks for all that enlightening information and encouragement, sister dear," Annabelle grumbled through the door.

"You're welcome!"

9...

Vic DeMarr blocked Annabelle's way into her Spanish class.

"You girls missed the *Weathervane* meeting yesterday," he said. "Sylvia said it was because you were busy working on the interview you got." He snickered.

Annabelle tried to ignore him, but he ducked his head down and looked into her face.

"You got it, didn't you, Goobitz?"

"Since when do I report to you, DeMarr?" Annabelle said, looking right back at him.

"Don't you want to know what you missed at the meeting?"

"Mr. Hedley knew we were working and wouldn't be there. Besides, Jo sold six ads already and he's thrilled to death. Now, can I go into Spanish?"

"You didn't get it, didja? You didn't meet him. Didja?"

Annabelle smiled her sweetest smile and spoke in her sweetest voice. "Would you like to do this story with us, Vic?" she asked.

He cocked his head, frowned at her. "You're kidding, aren't you?" When she grinned back, he growled, "You didn't meet him, you'll *never* meet him, you're just *hot dogs*, Goobitz!" and stalked off.

Annabelle would have laughed if she weren't afraid he might be right.

JOURNAL ENTRY 6:
We're all together again and ready to crash Subject's building. The first thing to do is get by Subject's doorman and meet Subject's neighbor. This may be almost as hard as meeting Subject Himself.

"*This* time, we don't approach in a bunch," Annabelle said. "One of us will just go up to the doorman and say she's here to walk Mrs. Whatsername's dog."

"Whitehead-Lake."

"Yeah. Whitehead-Lake. Sounds like a resort in the Poconos."

"Good idea," Josephine said. "All we need to do is find out what floor Hap's on, so there's no chance of only one of us meeting him. I'm sure he's rehearsing, anyway."

"Right. And if there's any trouble, four of us can distract the doorman while the other one sneaks in."

"Oh, boy," Helaine said.

"Does anyone want to volunteer?"

"I guess you do, Annabelle," Dorothy said. "We'll wait on the corner."

Annabelle approached the entrance to seven-twenty-four East Sixty-fifth Street. She saw the doorman sitting on a stool against the wall under the maroon awning. He was wearing his fall uniform: a long tan overcoat decorated with gold braid and a cap to match.

Doormen, Annabelle sighed to herself. We don't seem to have any luck with doormen.

But she said brightly, "Hello!"

"Hello," the doorman answered. "May I help you?"

"Yes, I'm to see Mrs. Alexandra Whitehead-Lake. I'm going to walk her dog."

"Sure." The doorman rose from the stool. "I'll phone up."

"Uh—wait—"

"Something wrong?"

Annabelle shuffled her feet. "No, but—the thing is, she doesn't know me. See, I'm just applying for the job. So if you phone up to her . . . she won't recognize the name."

The doorman looked at Annabelle. "Well," he said,

"I can't let you up without phoning first. So what do you want to do?"

Annabelle thought. "Suppose you phone her and say there's a girl here who wants to apply for the job of walking her dog. Maybe that'll be okay."

He shrugged and went inside to his call board. Annabelle followed him and gasped. All the names are here! she thought, pushing a knuckle against her lips. Why didn't we think of that? He's got all the names on that board!

But the board was in a little office and Annabelle couldn't get in. She peered at the rows of tenants' names and their apartment numbers as hard as she could, but the print was too small. She couldn't make out even one name.

"Sorry. She's busy," the doorman said. "And she wants to walk her dog herself. Wants to know how you got her name."

"Oh, I'm enterprising," Annabelle said quickly. "I need a job after school, so I check out all the dogs I can in the neighborhood."

"Yeah. Well, people get nervous when strangers know their names in this city. Can't be too careful."

"Right. Thanks anyway," Annabelle said and quickly left the building.

"Well?"

"No luck with Mrs. A. W-L. But there's a list of names of all the tenants right in the doorman's little office."

"I knew that," Josephine said. "But you can't read

105

them. They're practically on microfilm, for Pete's sake. A doorman won't let strangers see the tenants' names."

"We have to distract him, that's all," Annabelle said.

Helaine said, "Oh, boy . . ."

"How about if Dorothy faints?"

"No. Absolutely not. No more of that stuff. You all saw how well it worked last time," Dorothy said, backing away.

"One of us will have to get in that office," Annabelle said, "while the other three take up all the doorman's attention."

Shirley said, "Three? Did you say the other *three*, Annabelle?"

"I can't show my face again," Annabelle said. "It's not that I'm afraid, but he's already seen me. If I'm included in the distracting group then he'll suspect something."

"Then that means you're the one who sneaks in to read the names?" Helaine asked.

"I can't. I told you. He's seen me. We can't take the chance of his catching even a glimpse of me again. No. What I'll do is this: I'll go into the building next door and give out with a tremendous *geshrai*."

"It's Yiddish," Helaine said to the others. "It means scream. *Scream?*"

"Scream. You are all just casually walking by, da-da, da-da, da-da, when you hear this *geshrai* coming from the building and you rush in. What I say is, 'O my gosh, a mugger has just come out of this building with a lady's pock-et-book, whatever shall we *do?*' and you three say, 'Goodness, gracious, we will get help!' and you quick run next door, tell the doorman, he'll come over there to help you while I get out of the way fast and the fifth girl rushes into the office and reads the names. Foolproof."

"Foolproof," Helaine sighed.

"Do we have anything to lose?" Annabelle demanded.

"Face," Josephine said. "I'll be embarrassed to death."

"Who's going to do the sneaking in?" Helaine asked. "I'm too big. For once, I'm glad I'm fat."

"I'll do it," Shirley said.

"Good girl, Shirl!" Annabelle cried. "Okay. Ready?"

They looked at each other and giggled.

"Ready," Josephine said. "Listen to my heart. It's thumping out of my chest."

"Let's go."

Annabelle stood inside the vestibule of the building next door, a small apartment house with an untended lobby. Josephine, Dorothy and Helaine scurried to the far corner and then casually began to saunter back again. Shirley crossed the street in the other direction, prepared to enter seven-twenty-four from behind. There were hardly any people on the sidewalks. The signs were all favorable. Annabelle opened the door a crack in order to hear her friends' footsteps approaching.

There they were.

Tap, tap, tap . . .

"YAAAAAAAAAAAAAHGH!" Annabelle screeched at the top of her lungs. And then she rushed out of the building to find a place to hide.

The three girls ran into the vestibule for a moment,

then raced out again toward seven-twenty-four. The doorman was off his stool.

"Hey! What's going on over there?" he asked.

"It was a mugging!" Dorothy cried, pointing to the building next door.

"Someone took a lady's pocketbook!" Helaine told him.

"You better come over right away!" Josephine said, taking his arm.

"Yeah. Yeah, okay," the doorman said. "You know, I thought I saw someone running out of there. There was a girl here before. Said she was looking to walk dogs. I bet that was a scam. Well, I got a pretty good description of that kid . . ."

"No! It was a man!" Helaine cried, looking at the others. "The lady said it was a man. Big! Huge! A huge man! This tall!" She held up her arm and jumped into the air.

The four of them ran next door as Shirley slipped through seven-twenty-four's glass doors unseen.

"She's gone," Helaine wailed to the doorman. "We left her right here. We said we were going to get help."

"Where *could* she have gone?" Josephine said, looking around the tiny vestibule.

"She's not here now," the doorman said. "I've got to get back to my building—"

"No, wait! Just one second," Dorothy said. "Please— the lady was so scared . . . We're just kids . . . You're a man—so much more reassuring—"

Josephine made a face at Dorothy behind the doorman's back.

"Listen, girls," the doorman said, "she's not here. If you see her, bring her to me next door and we'll see if we can get a description. Are you girls witnesses?"

"Oh, no, we didn't see anything."

"Well, yeah, but if someone ran out of the building, you would have seen him, wouldn't you? I mean, you were right there when she screamed."

"Maybe he never left the building!" Josephine said quickly. "Maybe he's still here!"

"And maybe it was that kid," the doorman said. "Because I could have sworn I saw a kid running out of here after that scream . . ."

"We didn't see any kid. At all. No one. At all," Helaine said.

The doorman frowned suspiciously.

"That's all the time I got," he said. "I'm going back to work." He stepped out of the vestibule, followed by the girls.

Josephine and Dorothy hung back as the doorman resettled himself on his stool in front of seven-twenty-four.

"Did Shirley have enough time in there?" Dorothy whispered.

"I hope so. I want to get out of this neighborhood!" Josephine whispered back.

The doorman, on his stool, peered around.

No sign of Shirley.

Helaine, Josephine and Dorothy looked up and down the street, checking for a glimpse of either Shirley or Annabelle.

"Forget it," the doorman said. "He got away. Or she. Or anyone . . ."

"I guess . . ." Josephine said and smiled weakly at him.

Suddenly, the glass doors of seven-twenty-four swung open and Shirley walked out.

"Hi, George," she said to the doorman.

"Uh, hello—"

"You remember me," Shirley said. "Mr. Forsythe's niece. I visited here before."

"Yeah. Hi."

"Bye now," Shirley chirped and walked off down the block without a glance at the three girls staring at her with their mouths open.

Waving to the doorman, they walked slowly away.

"Where's Shirley *going?*" Helaine whispered.

"Probably to the corner, where she'll turn and then wait for us. Walk slowly. Slow-er! Don't let him think we're all together!"

"Where's *Annabelle?*"

"Lord knows. Do you know how close she came to getting arrested? And *she* was the one who couldn't be seen!"

"Why did she run out of the building that way?"

"Because she couldn't be standing in that vestibule when we came back with the doorman, that's why!"

They came to the corner. Shirley was there, pressed against the building.

"Is the coast clear?" she asked.

"She thinks she's 'The Rockford Files,' " Josephine sighed. "We're all seeing a new side of you, Shirley."

"How'd you know the doorman's name was George?" Helaine demanded. "And *who's* Mr. Forsythe?"

110

"I knew the doorman's name was George because there was a nameplate thing on his desk. And I don't know who Mr. Forsythe is, except that was one of the tenants' names I read. That's not hard. Anyway, I was just finishing scanning the whole list when you got back. So I had to say something when I walked out of the building or how would it look?"

"Well, you were terrific, Shirl," Josephine said and clapped her on the shoulder. "So *cool!* Walking out of there like you owned the place."

"Where's Annabelle?" Shirley asked.

"We don't know!"

"If she's smart, she went home," Josephine said.

"Annabelle would *not* go home," Helaine said.

"No, you're right. Here she comes."

Annabelle approached them from the opposite corner. Her face was purple and she was panting.

"Where were you?" Dorothy asked.

"I ran around two long blocks and came in from the other direction," she panted. "I think I'm dying."

"Do you know the doorman thought it was you who stole the lady's pocketbook? He thought he saw you running out of the building," Helaine said. "He was ready to have you arrested!"

"Oh, gosh . . ." Annabelle tried to catch her breath. "I was hoping I could get away before he got off his stool . . . Anyway, I *couldn't* get arrested. There was no lady and there was no pocketbook!"

"Oh. That's right," Helaine said.

They all leaned against the wall, Annabelle breathing heavily.

"Whew," she said finally. "Well, that was fun, wasn't it."

"Yeah," Shirley said, smiling. "It really was."

Suddenly, Josephine pulled herself away from the wall.

"Hey!" she cried.

"What?"

"What *happened?*"

"To whom?"

"With the *names*, you dummies!"

They began to laugh.

"Of course! The names! I nearly forgot!" Helaine said, slapping her thighs. "Shirley, did you find Hap Rhysbeck's *name?*"

"No."

"*NO?*" It was a chorus.

"I read every name. I *did*," Shirley insisted. "It wasn't there."

"Oh, broth-er!" Annabelle leaned back against the wall.

"I didn't miss one," Shirley said. "And Hap Rhysbeck wasn't there."

"He probably moved," Helaine wailed. "Big stars do that all the time! He's probably moved about four times already since that appendix operation last June—"

Josephine sighed. "All that for nothing," she said.

"Well . . . but it was fun," Shirley said. "Wasn't it?"

● ● ●

"We've come to a dead end, you know," Annabelle said on the subway home. "And I just hate it. I keep seeing Vic DeMarr's sneering face. And we let the school down, too."

"No, we didn't," Josephine said. "Mr. Hedley said the story of 'tracking the star' would be good, too. Unusual, he said."

Dorothy began to cry.

"Oh, Dottie, come on," Shirley said, patting her arm.

"B-But I was counting on it," Dorothy sniffed. "I just knew we were going to actually meet him and now all I have is my p-posters . . ."

"Well . . . we learned a lot . . . Didn't we?" Helaine asked.

"We learned a lot about *Shirley*," Josephine said. "Boy, Shirl—you gotta watch those quiet ones."

"It was so much fun," Shirley said.

"Yeah," Annabelle agreed, "but we didn't make a name for ourselves after all . . ."

"Annabelle, maybe our story will help *Weathervane* win the contest. We do have a lot of stuff to write. All the things we did . . ."

"Phooey," Annabelle mumbled.

"Let's get something to eat at Goobitz's," Helaine suggested. "We deserve it. And we can start to write our story. Shirley has her notes."

They all got off the train near the delicatessen. They hardly spoke as they walked. The little bell tinkled brightly over the door as they entered the shop and heard Rosalyn singing.

"Is that Rosalyn?" Helaine asked Annabelle. "Singing?"

"She sings all the time now," Annabelle answered. "In the shower, at breakfast, in the deli—it's obnoxious."

"Well, if it isn't the quintet," Rosalyn chirped. "Where have you all been. Helaine's?"

They sank into a booth near the counter.

"I want a hot pastrami on rye," Helaine said. "And two pickles. And cole slaw. And a root beer."

"Now, Helaine . . ." Dorothy said, but Helaine ignored her.

"We'll all share that," Annabelle said to Rosalyn. "Put it on my tab."

"Your tab," Rosalyn said with a smile and went on singing "I Get a Kick Out of You."

When she brought the plate to their table, Dorothy gaped at her.

"Rosalyn, did you do something to your hair?" she asked.

"Uh-huh. I had it cut and frosted."

"And how do you like the eye shadow?" Annabelle said. "It's called Midnight Baby. My sister looks like a before-and-after ad."

"I think she looks wonderful," Shirley breathed. "And she didn't even take my mother's course!"

"See what love can do?" Annabelle said as Rosalyn grinned at her. "She doesn't even mind my put-downs any more."

"Love is making *me* a wreck," Dorothy sighed. "You're lucky, Roz . . ."

"I know!"

"How come we haven't met him?" Josephine asked. "I still think it's Fred."

"Believe me, it's not Fred," Rosalyn said. "And you will meet him as soon as all your schedules permit. Even Annabelle hasn't met him yet." She went back behind the counter.

"Really?"

"It would make me question his existence if my mother weren't so ecstatic about the whole thing," Annabelle said. "Listen, why don't we get out the notes and start to write this thing. I want to get it over with. Our failure is depressing me. Tomorrow we have to face Vic DeMarr. And Sylvia Goldberg! Now *she* believed in us! I feel awful . . ."

"I thought of a way to cheer us up," Dorothy said. "And get one last crack at Hap."

The four others looked up.

"Let's go to the show Saturday night."

"You're crazy, Dot."

"Don't you want to? Wouldn't that be fun? And maybe afterward try to go backstage . . ."

"*Forget* it!" Josephine said. "Never will I go back there again. And Saturday night? Do you know the kind of chance we stand? Zip-po!"

"Okay, okay . . ."

"Let's do that," Shirley said. "Let's at least all go to the show."

"Right," Josephine said, her lips twisted into a sneer. "Now, Shirl, you've come a long way, but slow down, honey. Whose parents are going to let us go to a television show in this city all by ourselves at eleven-thirty at night? Not to mention that we'll probably never even get near the door, it gets so mobbed with people standing on line for last minute tickets . . . . Now let's use our heads, shall we?"

Dorothy said, "Sh!"

"What?"

"I said 'sh!' I don't want Rosalyn to hear us. And Mr. and Mrs. Goobitz could come out front here any minute. So, sh! We can do it." She bent over the table. All the others leaned in.

"We tell our parents—" She looked around to see if anyone was close by. No one was. "We tell our parents we're going to one of our houses for a slumber party. We do that all the time. They know that. And then— we just go!"

"Even if we did that," Josephine said, "what happens when it's over? We can't all go home. We're supposed to be at someone's house. Right?"

"Oh, that's no problem. We'll just go to each other's houses in one pair and one threesome. We'll say we had a fight or something and decided to go to another house. Our parents won't be mad because we didn't walk the streets by ourselves. It'll work. We'll be in someone's house by one-thirty the latest."

"I think you're crazy," Josephine repeated.

"After today, we *know* we're crazy," Annabelle said. "I say let's do it."

10...

"Ma, I'm going to Helaine's for a slumber party to-night," Annabelle said on Saturday.

"Okay . . . You can have it here if you want . . . Rosalyn's going out."

"No-o-o, I don't think so. Helaine's got it all planned. Where's Roz going?"

"She didn't say."

"And don't you *care?*"

"Annabelle Goobitz, of course I care. But she's going with Harvey and I've seen him enough times to trust him. He's such a lovely boy!"

"Well, maybe I'll get to meet him finally. Before I go to Helaine's."

"I don't think so, Annabelle. He's working on Saturday so Rosalyn will have to pick him up there."

"Oh, great," Annabelle sighed.

"Mama, I'm going to Josephine's for a slumber party tonight," Shirley said on Saturday.

"Josephine's?"

"Uh-huh . . ."

"Why don't you bring the girls here for a change, Shirley?" her mother asked. "You're always going there."

"I know, but there are five of us. Jo's place is mammoth."

"Even with all those relatives?"

"Oh, yes. There's lots of room. And her living room's huge, there's room for all our sleeping bags."

"Josephine's, eh?"

"Yup."

"Well, all right . . ."

"Mom, I'm going to Shirley's for a slumber party tonight," Helaine said that morning.

"Shirley's? Have you gone there before?"

"Well, we all decided we needed a change."

"That's nice . . . But I like it when the girls are here."

"I know, Mom . . . so you can keep track of what I eat."

"Now, Helaine . . ."

"I won't eat. Much."

"Do I do this for me? Helaine, is it for myself?"

"I *swear!* I'll bring dried fruits!"

"*I'll* pack your food. Mrs. Ferguson will cook it for you."

"Oh, Mom, I'll cook it myself. I promise. Can I go?"

"I guess so . . ."

"Ma, I'm going to Dorothy's for a slumber party tonight," Josephine said, once she located her mother in the large apartment.

"You have to? I thought we'd take Aunt Ramona and the boys to a movie."

"You can go. I want to go to Dot's."

"But you explain the movies to Aunt Ramona better than I do."

"Come on—*you* speak much better Italian than I do."

"Of course, but does she listen to me? *You* she understands."

"Let Fred explain the movie."

"Fred, he's going out. A college party or something."

"Is he taking Rosalyn Goobitz?" Josephine asked.

"Rosalyn Goobitz? How should I know? Say, that'd be nice, Josephine . . ."

"Yeah . . ."

"So. You won't come to the movies?"

"I'd really rather go to Dot's tonight. Next week I'll go with you. Okay?"

"La famiglia è tutto, Josefina," her mother said. But she smiled.

"Mom, I'll be at Annabelle's tonight for a slumber party," Dorothy said at lunch.

"Not till your room is cleaned."

"Oh, Mom, it is clean. It's just the way I like it."

"Dottie, I can live with posters on the walls. Maybe. But on your headboard? Your closet door? The windows? The mirror? And all the *same one?* Something has to go, Dorothy."

"Mother, I want to face Hap Rhysbeck every time I move. It's *my* room."

"Why couldn't you pick someone more like Warren Beatty?" her mother asked. "This one is so—so sleazy-looking!"

"Moth-er!"

"Well . . ."

"I think Warren Beatty is *ug.*"

Dorothy's mother held out her hands and looked at the ceiling.

"If I take the posters off the windows, can I go?"

"You can go. You can even *stay* if you replace them with Warren Beatty."

"Thanks, Mom!"

"Even Robert Redford. Dorothy?"

They met at seven-thirty at a Burger King a few blocks from Goobitz's delicatessen.

120

"We'd better get going," Annabelle said. "We'll be standing on line for hours."

"What I'd like to know is, what are we going to do with our overnight stuff?" Josephine said.

"And sleeping bags," Dorothy said.

"And this food," Helaine said, holding up a paper sack. "There are two raw lamb chops in here."

"Uh. Yeah . . . What'll we do with all this?"

"Leave it with the doorman," Josephine said, but no one laughed.

"We could rent a locker . . . At the train station . . . or something," Shirley suggested.

"Too out-of-the-way. And then we'd have to go back there. At one o'clock in the morning. No."

"We'll just have to take it, that's all," Dorothy said. "What else can we do?"

"Besides, it'll keep us warm while we're waiting on line. We can wrap up in the sleeping bags."

"And build a fire and cook the lamb chops . . ."

"Come on! We're wasting time!"

The line for tickets to "Live From Sound Stage 3" wasn't too long when the girls arrived at eight o'clock. They bundled themselves into their sleeping bags and took turns going out for food and hot drinks.

"I feel better," Dorothy said, "knowing he's just beyond that door."

When the time came for letting the crowds in, there was a huge crush at the door. Clutching each other and all their overnight gear, they squeezed through along

121

with hundreds of other young people and raced together to find seats in the immense studio.

"Ow!" Dorothy screamed. "Oh, no . . ."

"What?"

"Someone stepped on my foot . . . I lost my gym bag . . ."

"But we can't stop! We'll never get seats!"

"But it had my Mickey Mouse nightgown in it," she wailed.

"Dottie Pevney, do you want to see Hap Rhysbeck or do you want to go back and look for your Mickey Mouse nightgown?"

Dorothy gritted her teeth and pushed on.

"Good-eeee, we're way down front!" Helaine squealed excitedly. "We can see every pore on their faces!"

"Don't you love this?" Shirley cried. "Dottie, where did you tell your parents you'd be?"

"Oh, gosh—I forget! Where'd you?"

"Jo's," Shirley answered.

"Only my father's home," Jo said. "I hope they don't call."

"Let's *everybody* hope nobody calls," Annabelle said, "or we're all in trouble."

"No one will call. They never call. Annabelle . . ." Josephine said, "did Roz go out tonight?"

"Yeah. Why?"

"Did you meet Harvey?"

"No, she had to meet him at work. Why, Jo?"

"Fred didn't come home all afternoon. He was meeting his date, too . . ."

122

Josephine and Annabelle looked at each other and grinned.

The show, they all agreed, was one of "Sound Stage 3" 's best. The five girls laughed, screamed, nudged, elbowed and poked each other. They followed the monitor when they couldn't see the action from where they were sitting and loved it just as much.

"Look!" Annabelle squealed as a new sketch began.

"What?"

"What?"

Annabelle pointed. "Would you look at those costumes? Do you know what they're doing?"

Josephine gasped. "They're doing *munchkins!*"

"They sure are! They look just like we did last week!"

"I swear that's my mother's brown wig!" Helaine cried.

"And my Mexican vest!" Shirley yelled.

"Sh!" someone behind them said, leaning forward.

"They copied us!" Helaine said. "They copied just what we looked like and now they're doing munchkins! Boy!"

Annabelle leaned back in her seat and grinned. "They took their idea right from us," she said proudly. Then she frowned. "They should give us credit!"

"Sh! Watch the sketch," Josephine said.

They did. The audience howled, but the girls were critics.

"We could have done it better," Annabelle mumbled.

123

"Sure we could have," Shirley said. "It was ours in the first place."

"Let's go back next week wearing something else," Annabelle said and Josephine glared at her.

It was at the very end, during the last commercial break, that the girls began to feel a little nervous.

"We've got to leave as soon as it's over," Helaine whispered.

"Oh, can't we even try to go backst—" Dorothy began, but Josephine clapped a hand over her mouth.

"Don't you ever give up?" Josephine said.

"Where will we go?" Shirley asked.

"Okay—Dottie and Jo come with me to my house," Annabelle said.

"I can't do that. I'm supposed to *be* at Dot's. Helaine, *you* go to Annabelle's."

"No, I said *I* was going to Helaine's," Annabelle said.

"Oh, my gosh—" Helaine groaned, but Dorothy said, "Sh! Quiet! They're coming back to sign off!"

"Wow, it was a good show," Josephine sighed, smiling again.

"Look at Hap in that bunny costume. Isn't he the cutest?" Dorothy said.

"We want to thank Jim, our wonderful guest host this week—" Hap Rhysbeck said as the music played softly behind him, "and that absolutely fantastic group, Slop Bucket—what a sound, hey, folks?" The audience cheered. "And now, before we leave y'all for another week, I have a little announcement to make, right here on live television!" The music stopped. The rest of the cast looked bewildered.

124

"This isn't part of it," Annabelle whispered. "Is it?"

"I don't think so . . ."

"I would like to introduce to my fellow performers"—Hap, grinning took a mock bow—"and to the crew and to the WORLD—*the* future MRS. HAP RHYSBECK!" He held out his arm toward the backstage area.

Josephine reached instinctively for Dorothy, who was gasping for air.

"Come on," Hap was saying offstage. "Please. Come out."

"He's begging some girl to come out," Annabelle said.

"I don't believe this. It's a gag," Helaine said.

"It's part of the show, it's got to be," Josephine said. "Dorothy, it's a *gag!* Annabelle, I think she's having a heart attack."

"I'm fainting," Dorothy gasped, putting her head down.

Hap Rhysbeck had gone to the back of a set and was tugging on someone's arm. A spotlight suddenly focused directly on him as he succeeded in dragging the reluctant future Mrs. Hap Rhysbeck onto the set.

Suddenly, Annabelle was on her feet.

"I'm fainting," Dorothy moaned.

"It's a *bit,* Dorothy," Shirley was saying. "He doesn't mean it . . ." She stopped as someone fell hard against her. "Annabelle!" she cried. But Annabelle had slumped down to the floor. "Annabelle!" Shirley cried again. "Jo, what's the matter with Annabelle?"

"The matter with Annabelle is that the future Mrs. Hap Rhysbeck is none other than Rosalyn Goobitz."

"Rah—Rah—" Dorothy stammered.

"She's cheering," Helaine said.

"It really *is* Rosalyn up there," Shirley said, wide-eyed. "It really *is.*"

"Annabelle's really fainted, too," Josephine said, pulling at Annabelle's waist. "Hey! Hey, somebody! Help! Can anyone help us?"

The cameras had stopped rolling as the show ended with a spotlight on Hap Rhysbeck beaming at the audience, the cast and crew applauding, the audience screaming and Rosalyn, looking terrified, with Hap's arm around her waist. No one heard Josephine crying for help, but Hap, looking down, saw the girls, their expressions and an inert Annabelle now slumped in a seat. He leaped toward them from the low-platformed stage.

"It's okay," he said, pushing Josephine and Shirley aside, "I know CPR. Move over, please, everybody—" He bent over, grabbed Annabelle and moved her into the aisle, where he put her down flat. People stood up, leaned over their seats, pushed each other for a better view.

"Would you all just stand back, please?" Josephine cried. "Please! Could you all move back!"

Annabelle, on the floor in the aisle, opened her eyes.

She saw two pink bunny ears bobbing into her face and gluey-looking whiskers coming toward her mouth. Suddenly the big bunny's mouth was on hers and she felt air being pushed into her lungs. Her eyes opened wider.

"She's awake!" Helaine said, peering down. "You can stop! She's awake!"

126

Hap Rhysbeck pushed himself back.

"Hi," he said, smiling down at Annabelle. "You okay?"

Annabelle stared at him.

"You fainted when I announced my engagement," Hap explained.

Annabelle stared. She opened her mouth.

"You remember?" Hap asked.

"You're not a bunny," she said. "You're Hap Rhysbeck."

"That's right. And you're—?"

"Annabelle Goobitz."

"—Goobitz?"

"That's right."

"Yeah!" Dorothy cried. "Annabelle Goobitz getting *my* kiss!"

Suddenly, there was Rosalyn, bending over Annabelle.

"What are you *doing* here?" she demanded.

"Fainting over what *you're* doing here," Annabelle snapped, raising herself up on her elbows. Rosalyn reddened and looked around.

"Let's get her out of here," she said to Hap. "Let's get out of this crowd!"

They helped Annabelle to her feet and all of them went backstage to Hap's dressing room, with Rosalyn and Annabelle yelling at each other the entire time, oblivious to the amusement and confusion of the crowd.

"You're engaged?" Annabelle screamed. "To a big famous star? You never said anything?"

127

"I'm *not* engaged! And I never knew he was who he was until today!"

"What about Harvey?" Annabelle cried.

"This *is* Harvey," Rosalyn screamed. "That's his real name. He came to the deli on Sunday! He loved the Good Bits platter you sent him! He wanted our food! But he didn't want to be recognized, so he came as his real self. Harvey Ryzbecski! It wasn't until today that he told me who he was!"

"But—but—" Annabelle stammered.

"He picked me up in a rush this afternoon. He said he was on his break, that he had a surprise for me. I was surprised, all right!"

"I'll bet," Dorothy said, her lip trembling.

"Well, I *was!* You can imagine," Rosalyn said. "He told me who he was, let me watch the rehearsal—he said he just wanted to be *himself* in the outside world. Himself! Harvey Ryzbecski is a wonderful, sweet, quiet boy! I've been in a daze all afternoon! But I never thought he'd pull a stunt like this!" She glared at Hap who had been trying to speak. His arms were stretched toward her.

"Rosalyn—" he began.

"Well, Harvey Ryzbecski didn't pull this," Rosalyn interrupted. "Hap Rhysbeck did! They're certainly two very different people!"

Hap looked pained. "Rosalyn—" he said again.

"Just like *Sybil*," Shirley breathed. "Remember that movie?"

"Come on," Rosalyn said. "We're going home." She stood up.

128

"Tell me, Mr. Rhysbeck," Josephine said, "when did you discover these two personalities lived inside you?"

"Oh, Lord, she's interviewing him," Helaine moaned.

"It's our only chance," Josephine said, and turned back to Hap. "Where were you born? When did you know you wanted to be a performer? Where did you go to school?"

"Hey, wait—Roz, please," Hap was saying, as Rosalyn began to help Annabelle gather her things. "Listen, Roz, I never thought you'd take it like this. I thought you'd be flattered. I thought you'd appreciate—"

"Flattered! I'll show you what I appreciate, Mr. Rhysbeck," Rosalyn growled.

"Were you the class clown?" Josephine asked. "Where do your parents live? How do they feel about your success? Do you *really* want to marry Rosalyn?"

In the commotion, Josephine's sleeping bag was stolen, the contents of Annabelle's backpack were strewn over the first three rows of the audience and Helaine lost her lamb chops. Rosalyn got all the girls into two taxis and had the drivers take them to the Goobitz's.

Dorothy sobbed softly, sitting next to Annabelle in the first cab.

"Oh, Dottie, don't cry . . . We'll fix it with our parents. After all, Rosalyn was there. We were chaperoned . . ."

"That's not why I'm crying," Dorothy wailed. "He kissed you, Annabelle! You stole *my* faint and it was *you* he kissed!"

"He didn't *kiss* me, Dorothy, he was giving me CPR! There's a big difference, Dorothy. You don't have to *know* someone for them to give you CPR!"

"But it should have been me! Now every time I fantasize Hap Rhysbeck in a passionate embrace it's going to be with *you!*"

Rosalyn laughed drily.

In the other cab, Helaine nudged Josephine.

"Did he answer *any* of your questions, Jo?" she asked.

"Not one. He was too busy following Rosalyn. And pleading with her. I don't even think he heard me."

"Imagine. Rosalyn walked out on him! Imagine. Rosalyn Goobitz walked out on Hap Rhysbeck! In front of a thousand people!"

"It's been a strange night," Josephine said and suddenly started to laugh.

"What's funny?" Shirley asked.

Josephine covered her giggles with her hand.

"I thought it was Fred!" she said, her shoulders shaking. "All this time I thought it was Fred!"

Dragging their gear and leaning on each other for support, the five girls slogged down the corridor toward the Goobitz's apartment. Rosalyn walked ahead of them, her face still red and angry-looking. As they neared the door, they could hear the phone ringing and Leonard Goobitz yelling.

"Oh, no," Annabelle groaned. "What now?"

Rosalyn opened the door with her key. Her mother and father, in bathrobes and pajamas, were standing in the foyer. Leonard Goobitz was holding a phone. Both of them turned and stared at the group in the doorway with confused expressions on their faces.

"What's going on?" Miriam said at the same time Rosalyn asked, "What's going on?"

"What's going on is the phone hasn't stopped ringing for the last half hour!" Leonard Goobitz screamed. "Where were you? What are the kids doing here? Who's Hap Risnick? Newspapers, TV, people have been calling up in the middle of the night—"

Miriam Goobitz put her hands on her hips and glared at her older daughter. "Rosalyn Goobitz, *did you get married tonight?*" she screamed.

They took the phone off the hook while Rosalyn told her parents what had happened. Dorothy and Helaine fell asleep on the floor while Josephine, Shirley and Annabelle sat on the couch, listening to Rosalyn and staring at their laps.

Leonard Goobitz kept muttering "Ay, ay, ay," and, "Oy, oy, oy," and slapping the side of his face with his palm while Rosalyn talked.

"What, so he's not Harvey?" Miriam asked.

"Yeah, he is, but mainly he's Hap Rhysbeck," Rosalyn said, shaking her head. "He brought me to their rehearsal today. He asked wouldn't I have fun watching

131

the show from the wings. He said we'd go out afterwards. Who thought he'd pull me out there at the last minute that way? Embarrass me like that! I'm telling you, I've never been so furious!"

"And the kids? You took the kids?"

"Yes!" Annabelle said, shooting a look at Rosalyn. "It was a surprise. She took us! She was being nice. She's a good sister. Right, Roz . . .?"

Rosalyn sighed.

"I think I want to go home," Helaine muttered. Her eyes were still closed.

"Me, too," Dorothy said, leaning against her.

"Stay, girls," Miriam said. "It's too late to go home now. I'll get some blankets, some pillows—sleep. In the morning you'll go home."

They kept the phone off the hook.

11...

Reporters kept the Goobitz household in pandemonium the next day. Rosalyn was afraid to go to the deli and stayed home. Her mother and Annabelle stayed with her. Hap Rhysbeck tried to get through and succeeded twice. Rosalyn hung up on him once and Miriam once. Annabelle was in charge of anyone who actually got into their building and came to the door. Once, she threw an ashtray and chipped a piece of the door frame.

"And we thought *we* were persistent as reporters,"

she said to her mother. "They really don't let you alone!"

"I don't want to talk to anyone," Rosalyn said. Her eyes were red. Everything had seemed to hit her when the sun came up and she hadn't stopped crying.

"You did the right thing," her mother said and kept bringing her trays of food, which were left uneaten. "The right thing. He was a nogoodnik, to do that to you. And to think I trusted him."

"He was so nice as Harvey," Rosalyn wailed.

"I don't even want the interview now," Annabelle said. "Even if he did give me CPR. What he did to Roz was mean."

That Sunday, the only one in good spirits was Leonard Goobitz. The deli was mobbed all day.

The students at James K. Polk Junior High School had seen or heard about the closing bit on "Live From Sound Stage 3" Saturday night, but none of them associated it with Annabelle. No one had recognized Rosalyn Goobitz—Hap had never used her name—and his artificial resuscitation of Annabelle was done off camera, after the show was over. Annabelle wasn't sure if she was relieved or sorry. There had been enough attention over the weekend. But she and Josephine went to Mr. Hedley's homeroom as soon as school was over.

"Ugh, there's Vic DeMarr," Annabelle said as she stood in the doorway.

"Oh, who cares?" Josephine said. "Just tell him what happened. We have a good story, anyway. *Weathervane*'ll win the contest. No one has anything like this!"

They stepped into the room.

"Hi, girls," Mr. Hedley greeted them. "How's the interview progressing?"

"Yeah," Vic DeMarr said with a grin. "How's the interview pro-gress-ing?"

"Well . . ." Annabelle began.

"We all met Hap Rhysbeck," Josephine finished with a grin.

"Face to face," Annabelle added.

"Huh?" from Vic. "What?"

"But we didn't get any interview."

"Huh?" from Vic. "What?"

They told their story, while their teacher kept shaking his head and pulling on his chin.

"If you believe that, Mr. Hedley, you're—" Vic began, then waved his hand at them.

"You can check on the whole thing, DeMarr," Josephine said. "Believe me, it's all true."

"Your sister went out with Hap Rhysbeck?" Vic asked. He looked around at the crowd of kids who had gathered to listen to the story. "You mean, Goobitz, *your sister* went out with *Hap Rhysbeck?* That was *your sister* at the end of the show?"

"My *sister* went out with Harvey Ryzbecski," Annabelle said haughtily. "The fact that he turned out to be Hap Rhysbeck was not her fault."

"I think you're all terrific," Mr. Hedley said, smiling. "You go write that story you've gotten. I think it's a beaut. You write it just the way it happened, all of it. Just as soon as you can!"

"We will! Oh, we will, Mr. Hedley," Josephine cried.

"Hey, DeMarr—your mouth is open," Annabelle said as she turned to leave.

That afternoon, Adam's Ribbers met as usual at the Goobitz apartment. All of them, except for Annabelle, had slept until one o'clock on Sunday and were eager and excited about putting their newspaper article together. Even Dorothy had recovered.

"I still think he's cute," she said, "but he treated Rosalyn like dirt. He should have known she's not a show-off like he is. He didn't think of her feelings at all!"

"Right, Dot . . ."

"Still . . . *I'm* the one who would have fainted, if Annabelle hadn't done it first . . ."

"Come on," Shirley said, pulling her notes out of her school bag. "Let's start at the beginning and I'll take it down in my own shorthand. Everyone contributes what she remembers best, okay?"

"The CPR kiss!" Dorothy cried.

"Wait, that's last, Dottie . . ." She looked at her notes. "Okay, first was our phone call. To CBC."

"Right," Helaine said. "And then Fred's friend gave us the address of the studio!"

"But don't use his name!" Josephine cried. "Remember! Besides, reporters don't have to give their sources."

"And then the fainting!" Dorothy said. "And the doorman. And the Goobitz platter!"

"Oh, the Goobitz platter," Annabelle wailed. "That's what started it all."

"And the munchkins!"

"And the dog-walker!"

"And the robbery!"

Shirley was writing frantically.

"And don't forget Shirley's contribution, before we get any further," Josephine added. "Shirley, you write that part yourself. How you got the hospital records and the address and all."

"Well," Shirley said with a shrug, "it was the wrong address, though."

"Maybe not," Helaine said. "Maybe he was listed as Harvey Ryzbecski. Do you remember that?"

Shirley thought. "I don't know . . . I never looked for a Harvey Ryzbecski."

"See? Besides, it doesn't matter. It was good investigating on your part. But you'd better not mention the real address. We could get sued or something."

"I can write the part about the munchkins and the costumes," Dorothy offered. "I remember what everybody wore . . ."

"I'll do the stuff about the overnight things," Helaine said. "That was funny, dragging all that stuff around with us the night of the show . . ."

"Yeah, funny," Josephine said. "My sleeping bag got stolen. With everything that went on, *that's* what my mother's been harping on!"

"I'll do the part about the CPR," Annabelle said, "and about the ride home and the reporters and everything."

"Yeah, Annabelle," Dorothy said. "I'm sure that's your favorite part."

They spent the afternoon quietly, each girl in her own separate corner, each with part of Shirley's journal notes.

They managed to finish before supper and Shirley took all their work home to coordinate it.

"I'll bring it in tomorrow," Shirley said. "And we can submit it."

"This story is a winner," Helaine said. "The other schools might as well quit now!"

Sammy Prysock and Annabelle sat on the floor in a corner of the layout room at the printer's. In the center of the room was a large table under fluorescent lights, with copy in long strips draped over it. A man was putting strips together and cutting them.

"That must have been some wild night," Sammy said, shaking his head.

"It was," Annabelle said. "It was. The funny thing is, I think Hap Rhysbeck really meant it when he proposed to Rosalyn like that. But it doesn't matter. He really turned her off."

"You sure did some gutsy things, Annabelle," Sammy said. "You're a good reporter."

"Well, it was all of us, really," Annabelle said and fluffed her hair.

The man at the table interrupted them. "Hey, kids, something's gonna have to go, here," he said. "I don't have room for all of this article, 'On the Trail of—' "

"Oh, that's mine," Annabelle said from the floor.

"Well, you have to cut something from the first column—uh—'Our phone call to the studio seemed the most direct route, but—' "

138

"No, not that," Annabelle said.

The printer read on. " 'Shirley Ferguson tracked down the home address of—' "

"No, we can't cut any of that!"

"Well, look," the man said, "there's an ad at the bottom of the first column here and I'm sure you don't want that cut, right?"

Sammy said, "Oh, right. The ad stays." He smiled at Annabelle. "I'm still having a hard time believing all you girls did!" he said.

"Well, what goes then?" the man asked.

Annabelle sighed. "I just can't cut the copy. Can you pull out words or something? As long as the sentences make sense?" She was looking at Sammy.

The printer sighed. "Ah, I'll fix it," he said.

"I'm really going to have to do something about my grades now," Annabelle said. "I've hardly done any work in days and days."

"Oh, you'll catch up," Sammy said. "I wouldn't worry about it."

Annabelle felt herself blush.

"Well, I think we can go. Hedley left half an hour ago. They're about done." Sammy stood up and reached for Annabelle's hands. She smiled at him again as he pulled her to her feet.

Things were almost back to normal.

Adam's Ribbers held regular meetings and argued about sweater colors.

139

Helaine stuck to her diet, Shirley practiced her violin, Josephine teased her cousin Fred.

To her mother's relief, Dorothy took down all her Hap Rhysbeck posters. She left the spaces on her walls empty and waited patiently for a new crush.

Annabelle daydreamed about the newspaper story and helped out at the deli.

Only Rosalyn was different.

When it was learned that the engagement was not an engagement, and the news media finally left her alone, Rosalyn became a new person.

Hap Rhysbeck still came to Goobitz's Good Bits, but now he came as a friend, bringing all of *his* friends. The deli was a "show biz" hangout and Rosalyn was everyone's favorite chef-and-waitress. She kept all her makeup tricks and frosted hair; she bought new clothes; she smiled a lot. Now, everyone asked for Rosalyn's sandwiches and platters and she was greeted by television stars, movie stars, news reporters, writers, directors.

"Look, she's the 'Elaine' of the West Side," her father joked. "I should sell stock! We've never done better!"

Rosalyn dated a lot, too. But never anyone in show business.

The day the competing issue of *Weathervane* came out, the girls couldn't wait to get to school. Josephine was the first to grab a paper in the cafeteria.

"Where is it?" she muttered excitedly, thumbing pages.

"There's only six pages, Jo," Helaine said, peering over her shoulder.

140

"You went to the printer's when they did it, didn't you, Jo?" Dorothy asked. "How did it look?"

"I didn't go, I had to take Sebastian to the dentist. Annabelle went. Oh! Here it is! 'On the Trail of a Story and a Star,' " she read aloud, "by—by—*ANNA-BELLE GOOBITZ?*"

"What?" Helaine said.

"What?" Shirley said.

"What?" Dorothy said.

Annabelle said, "What?"

"Explain yourself, Goobitz!" Josephine yelled. Everyone in the cafeteria turned around. "Your stupid name is the only one on this story!"

Annabelle said, "I—"

"Annabelle, how could you do this?" Helaine said. "We all knew how badly you wanted fame, but to step on your friends on the way up the ladder of success—"

"Annabelle Goobitz, I just hope you're happy," Dorothy said, knocking the paper out of Josephine's hands to the floor. "I just hope you got what you wanted, but remember, Annabelle—*it's lonely at the top!*"

They stalked off. Only Shirley remained, staring open-mouthed at Annabelle.

"Annabelle?" she said finally. "You stink!"

Annabelle stared at Shirley's back, and her lower lip began to quiver.

Oh, wow, she thought. Oh, wow . . . I *really* blew it!

• • •

Absolutely no one would talk to her.

Annabelle went from class to class, meal to meal, from school to work to home—alone.

She began to hate the deli. Rosalyn's bright chatter and all the crowds depressed her. She tried to talk to each of her friends but no one would even look at her. Even though all of the five were mentioned throughout the story, the byline was Annabelle's alone and no one would forgive her for that. She spoke to Mr. Hedley, who said that they'd print a notice in the next issue to correct the error, but somehow Annabelle felt that wouldn't be enough. The competition entry had already been submitted. Her name was attached to it. That was that. No more meetings, no more slumber parties, no more friends.

After eight days of misery and loneliness, Annabelle decided drastic measures had to be taken.

The next Monday, she went to the school's office during sixth period.

"I'd like to use the P.A. system," she told the secretary.

"Sorry, Annabelle. Not without a written notice from a teacher."

"I *have* to use it," she said.

"Annabelle, you know the rules. Kids'd be in here all day using this thing if there were no authorization required."

"Okay," Annabelle said and hid outside in the hall until the secretary left the office. Then she sneaked in, threw the switch and picked up the microphone.

"Attention!" she yelled and the mike squealed loudly. She winced, coughed and spoke softer. "I'd like the attention of everybody in the whole school, but especially, Dottie and Jo and Helaine and Shirley! Now hear this!" She cleared her throat. "The story that is going to win the school newspaper award for James K. Polk Junior High School, the story called 'On the Trail of a Story and a Star,' was covered by *five people*. Not just one! Not just me, the way the byline says. It was all done by *five* people: Josephine Scarangillo, Helaine Jacoby, Dorothy Pevney, Shirley Ferguson and myself. What happened at the printer's was—one of the men said he'd have to cut something out of the first column because he didn't have enough space for all of the article and the ads, too. And the ads were important, after all, Josephine was the one who sold them. So I said—don't cut the part about the doorman or the fainting or the phone calls or any of that stuff. And he said, 'Okay then, what am I supposed to cut?' and I said back, 'You figure it out, but leave that story intact!' So what he ended up cutting was the five-line byline, leaving only my name, which happened to be first, sitting up there by itself. It wasn't my fault and I didn't ask for it and I want everyone to start speaking to me again—" Her voice cracked "—because I don't think fame is such a great thing after all. My sister Rosalyn won't even read *People* magazine any more after what she went through. And she could have had a nice boyfriend if he wasn't so famous . . . And I just want . . . my friends back . . . because you don't have to be *important* . . . to be im-

143

portant . . ." She sighed, clicked off the switch and looked up to see the school secretary glaring at her from the doorway.

"Sorry," Annabelle said. "I had to."

"So I see."

"Am I going to be suspended?"

"No," the secretary said. She bent over her desk and began to write. "Here," she said, when she was finished. "Put this in the box next to the microphone."

"What is it?" Annabelle asked.

"It's your written authorization," the secretary said.

"Sorry, Annabelle. We jumped to conclusions. We should have let you explain." Josephine put her arm around Annabelle.

"You were the one who went to the printer and you were the one who always wanted your name to go down in history . . ." Dorothy said. "Anyway, I'm glad we're friends again. I really couldn't stand it, trying to ignore you."

"I'm sorry I said you stink, Annabelle," Shirley said softly.

"Shirley Ferguson, did you really say that?" Helaine laughed.

"Well, I *did* go to the printer," Annabelle said, "and I really should have looked at what they did . . . Only I was talking to Sammy and I really wanted to wait and surprise myself when the paper came out for real. And Sammy was concerned mostly with the ads. I guess it

144

was my job to check it . . . I'm sorry. But anyway . . . we're best friends again. And that's what
counts!"

"La famiglia è tutto, Annabelle," Josephine said.

"Hey! Girls!"

They turned in the direction of the voice. It was
Sammy Prysock.

"Hi, Sam!" Annabelle called.

He came up to them. "Hi, Annabelle . . ." he said.

"What's new, Sam?" Dorothy asked.

"Uh . . ." Sammy looked at Annabelle and then at
the other girls. "The news is good and bad. The good
news is that the whole school is talking about your story
and Mr. Hedley wants you to talk to an assembly about
it. All of you." He smiled. "Is it okay?"

"Sure!" Josephine answered. "Great!"

"Oh, gosh, what'll I wear?" Helaine asked.

"Okay . . . What's the bad news, Sammy?" Annabelle asked, studying him.

"Well . . . Gee, Annabelle . . ."

"It's okay, Sammy, just tell us."

He sighed. "The bad news is, we have the results of
the competition. And *Weathervane* didn't win."

"*What?*"

"Let go of my shirt, Annabelle . . ."

"What do you mean we didn't win!" Dorothy demanded. "How could we not win? Who *did* win?"

"The *Colby Chronicle*," Sammy answered. "They did
a three-part series."

"On *what?*" Josephine demanded.

"It was an in-depth probe called 'Humanizing Your School Bus Driver.' "

"I'm calling this meeting to order formally," Annabelle began, "because we have to talk seriously about what we're going to say at the assembly."

"Let's each talk about our favorite part of the story," Helaine suggested. "And then kids can ask us questions."

"I think we should get our matching sweaters quick, so we can wear them," Josephine said. "Let's pick colors."

"No, let's talk about the whole point of the story," Annabelle said.

"Fame corrupts?" Dorothy asked.

"No, I don't think that's it."

"Goobitz makes the best food in town?"

"Uh-uh," Annabelle said. "I think the whole point is friendship. About how we worked together as friends. About how we couldn't have done it alone."

"Rosalyn could have done it alone," Dorothy muttered.

"Annabelle's right," Shirley said. "The main thing is how we all stuck together."

"Right."

"Hear, hear!"

"Okay. Now that's settled," Josephine said. "I still like powder blue and white."

"Too wishy-washy. Red and black," Dorothy said.

"Red and black is *vul*gar!" Josephine cried.

"How about navy blue and lavender?" Shirley suggested.

Annabelle sighed. "Have a cookie, Helaine," she said.

"Thanks," Helaine said and took one.